I, AN ACTRESS
THE AUTOBIOGRAPHY OF KAREN JAMEY

as told to
JEFFREY DINSMORE

contemporary press

This is a work of fiction. All of the characters and events portrayed
in this book are either products of the author's twisted imagination
or are used ficticiously.

I, An Actress

Cover Design by Dennis Hayes, Jennifer Lilya and Chris Reese

A Contemporary Press Book
Published by Contemporary Press
Brooklyn, New York

Distributed by Publishers Group West
www.pgw.com

www.contemporarypress.com

ISBN 0-9744614-9-0

Advance Copy 2005

Printed in the United States of America

I, AN ACTRESS

THE AUTOBIOGRAPHY OF KAREN JAMEY

as told to

JEFFREY DINSMORE

PROLOGUE

A Brief Word about Beginning a Historical Document

Were one to sit down and begin writing about one's life, one would first have to decide where one should begin. Does one begin at the very beginning, sliding down the birth canal head first, staring out into the crippling blindness of the operating room lights? I only wish I had that sort of memory at my disposal, birth memory being one of the most highly desired tools for a practicing member of my trade. What I wouldn't pay for the ability to recollect the terror and excitement of that pivotal moment in the history of cinema and the world. For to tell the story of my life is to tell the story of America, or, should I say, the America in which we live today, expunging the unnecessary 200 or so years before my birth, 300 if we care to date it all back to that initial voyage of Christopher Columbus. Although those who have studied American history in any sort of detail know that we can't really date it all back to then, what with there being a native culture on these shores for dozens if not hundreds of years before our arrival, and before that, some dinosaurs.

Or does one focus on a smaller moment, an incident that illustrates an important theme or arc of one's life story? I indeed have several such moments at my disposal, of which I can provide a small glimpse right now: the time that I skinned my knee under the blossoming juniper and the neighbor's dog, Stanchion, upon smelling the fresh child's blood that seeped from my open wound, gave me my first experience with unwarranted sexual desire; the time that I held the hand of a graying Mickey Rooney, former beloved child star, as he boarded a plane to the Republic of Tehran, inside of me a welling sadness at the realization that I would soon be parted from a man who I truthfully had little interaction with and who most likely knew little of me, yet seemed to appreciate the hand holding all the same; or that day in the mid-70s when, coming down from a three-day bender of reefer, pills, and pina coladas, I careened across the partition on Interstate 405, just outside of Encino, killing a small child and most of the joy inside of me in one, fell, dastardly swoop.

Does one begin on a sad note or a happy note? An exciting story that leaves the reader wanting more, or a mundane story to which anyone who has ever carried a lunch pail might relate?

When one is a highly respected actress who has been immortalized in several classic films, television series, and theatrical productions, the question of where to begin becomes doubly difficult. If I were, say, an automobile mechanic trying to pen a memoir, I might think, "Oh, that's easy! The day that I finally fixed that nasty transmission problem on the old Chevy is the perfect place to begin!" And that's all well and good, Mr. Auto Mechanic, sir; you have earned your brief moment of happiness and we don't fault you for clutching to that one sweet memory as a child might clutch to his mother's aching teat.

For those of us who have managed to carve out an existence of somewhat more significance, however, it is not quite so easy. Looking back upon the last sixty years of glamorous parties, torturous relationships, and dramatic flooferall, I am inclined to put the pen down right now and reach again for the sweet numbing bliss of the bottle, even though I am, in fact, not actually the one holding the pen. Nor is there a pen involved in the process at all, rather, it is a simple tape recording device into which I speak these words, later to be typewritten out by my editors ... or internetted ... or whatever it is they do nowadays.

Such a life I have lived, and such changes I have seen! Who could have thought, as a child in the 1920s, that we would now spend the day clacking away at our keyboards, creating virtual documents that are one electromagnet away from disappearing into the ether of non-existence? Who in 1926 would have presumed that a scrappy youngster from Baltimore would be cavorting with the rich and the ultra-rich in decadent palaces the world over, drenched in jewels and magnificent compliments and being seduced regularly by the most resplendent gentlemen to ever grace the pages of *Photoplay*? Certainly not I ... the questions proposed above being less about a generalized "who" character and more about myself.

Digressions, as my mentor Handy Peters often said, will get you everywhere. But in this case, I think the opposite is true. We must have a beginning, and we must have one now. If the history of movies did not begin with the Lumiere brothers and their fantastical moving film system, would there be a history of movies at all? Or would we be forced to sit in front of blank screens and project our own fantasies, create our own stories, entertain ourselves? I should think one would eventually say to oneself, "This movie-watching experience is not all it's cracked up to be!"

Thank God there is such a thing as movies, for if it were not for the movies, I would not be the woman that I am today. I don't know who I would be. Probably some kind of drooling mess standing on a street corner, screaming, "Give me a dollar, sir!" at the passing gentlefolk. Or I might be a washerwoman, pounding rugs with a broom and dreaming of the adventures I will never have. Thank God, indeed, that there is such a thing as movies, for without movies, I would most certainly not be what I am and what I was always meant to be: an actress.

Chapter One

Portrait of the Actress as a Young Girl

The ceilings are what I remember most of all.

The date ... I remember it like it was yesterday ... was October 6th, 1927, and my father and mother and I were seated in the front of the balcony for the debut of *The Jazz Singer* in Baltimore's brand-new luxury cinema, the Stanley. For one dollar and 35 cents, we were treated to 3 movie tickets, a large box of popcorn, 3 bags of penny candies, and 3 bottles of Mr. Creamy's Super Fizz. I had seen films before but had little interest in them ... it all just seemed like a bunch of dolts running around and getting hit with shovels, and since I couldn't even read the title cards, I couldn't quite understand why these characters continued to put up with such nonsense. If I were a construction worker and my boss hit me with a shovel, I would march right up to him and say, "I don't think so, Daddy." Since then, of course, my tastes have become somewhat more refined, and I now rather enjoy watching people get hit with shovels.

As I sat in that theater, waiting for the film to begin, I stared up at the ornate ceilings and hoped for this experience to be over soon.

I was born on April 30, 1922. In a twist of fate that would stand as an all-too-suitable metaphor for the story of my life, I was born a Hitler. Karen Jameson Hitler, to be more precise. This was, of course, years before the name Hitler would become synonymous with ultimate evil, and there were thousands of happy Hitler families just like mine living essentially hate-free lives all over America. Truth be told, my parents didn't much care for Jews, but I can assure you they never went so far as to lobby for genocide.

My childhood was, for the most part, quite a happy one. I was brought up in a small town just outside of Baltimore called Namsy Brooks. Don't look for it on a map; it's not there anymore. It was torn down in the early 1990s and replaced by a Wal-Mart. Such is the price of living in a civilized, progressive society. To this day, when I'm back in Baltimore, I always make certain to stop in the hunting goods section and think fondly back to the days when my tire swing arched over the area that is now home to cut-rate camouflaged jackets and Redi-Doe deer decoys.

My father was a salesman who made a decent, honest living traveling the country and selling mops to lonely housewives. He was a wise, caring man, and he always had a funny story or a song for me when I saw him, which, due to the unfortunate demands of the traveling salesman's life, was not very often in my formative years. I consider his absence a blessing, for in many ways it taught me to never depend on men for anything. I, of course, have contradicted that lesson with my behavior many times throughout the course of my life, but every time men fail me, I am at least able to tell myself that they're no better or worse than Daddy.

One thing that my father instilled in me early on was a love of entertainment. In my very early years, I was never a fan of the cinema, but I did grow up with a love for the theater that surpassed anyone I knew in my provincial town. Daddy's affection for the dramatic and comical did not materialize out of thin air; his parents were Rosalie and Seymour Hitler, a/k/a Nip n' Tuck, world-renowned stars of the Vaudeville stage. In fact, Daddy grew up in the glamorous world of show business and was planning on joining the family act until an unfortunate accident named "me" came into his life.

Daddy met Mother in a train station in Tallapoosa, Alabama, when he was just 15 years old and she a young ne'er do well of 18. He was in town with Granny and Granpapa on an extended stay at the popular Doc Polka's Theater of the Absurd and Medicine Show in downtown Tallapee.

Having lost his virginity to a crippled showgirl at the ripe age of 12, Daddy was a great admirer of the opposite sex, and so he would spend his afternoons at the train station, waiting to get first crack at the new girls arriving into town on the 12:10 and the 4:25. Charming and handsome as a bug, he'd introduce himself as the welcoming committee to the loveliest girls who caught his eye and provide them with free passes to the show that night.

The first time he saw Mother, so the story goes, he knew that she was to be his forever. He also knew that getting her to be his forever was going to be a formidable task, for at the time he met her, my mother was a hobo.

Although the word has come to have some fairly negative connotations, back in the teens and twenties, being a hobo wasn't such a bad career choice. Mother's parents had died at a young age, leaving her in the care of her older brother, an unsavory sort who made a living poaching cattle in the badlands of Texas. It wasn't long before this lifestyle caught up with him, and when she was just 14, her brother was sent off to the state pen for 8-10 years, leaving her on her own. It was then that she took to riding the rails. For the next four years, the boxcar transients became her family, the open rails her home. When I was growing up, she would regale me with tales of her adventures featuring characters like Stumpy Goodfella, the junkyard king, and Mama Miss Big Fat Pussy from Santa Fe. I would sit in the living room of our Namsy Brooks home in rapt attention, hardly imagining how someone so seemingly normal as Mother could get along in such a strange and exotic world. I was too young at the time to understand that my mother was anything but normal. Children don't understand normal, a trait that I have always admired in the children I meet. You could introduce a child to a two-headed purple creature from Mars and she would say, "Hello, sir, how do you do?"

If there's one thing my Daddy liked, it was a challenge, and he found it in Mother. She saw through his tired old approach immediately, and when he offered her tickets to the show, she politely told him to cram those tickets where the sun did not shine. Never missing a beat, Daddy pulled down his pants in front of a shocked audience at the crowded station and said, "Why don't you cram 'em there yourself, ma'am?" And so began a passionate, if ultimately ill-fated love affair that would rival the most spectacular romances ever captured on film.

Granny and Granpapa didn't take too kindly to Mother when Daddy brought her home, what with her being a dirty hobo, but I think they blamed themselves in some ways for failing to bring up a child with a rigorous moral system. They did love to help a person in need, though, and they invited her to stay with them in their small 2-bedroom apartment until she could get enough money to live on her own.

With only two bedrooms in the house, the consequences were inevitable. Although Mother was only planning on staying in Tallapee for a few days, she quite liked having a bed under her body and a man on top. To pay for her keep, Granny and Granpapa set her up with a job as a curtain puller for their show. Every night, she'd pull the curtains back to reveal Granny and Granpapa in black face and Daddy in the dress of a young dandy. Their classic routine, "The Dignified Gentry," was a real crowd pleaser, and people would come from miles around to see Daddy's hoity-toity young dandy character get his comeuppance from a couple of down-on-their-luck negroes.

The aughts being a more racially sensitive time, I feel it behooves me to mention a thing or two about the minstrel tradition from whence I spring. To some, minstrelsy is a quaint relic from a forgotten era; to others, it is a racist yak chained to the neck of popular American culture. My feelings lie somewhere in the middle. While I recognize that blackface is based in demeaning racial caricature, were it not for minstrelsy, we would not have a popular American stage, as it was the predominant form of theater from the 1860s all the way up through the Great Depression and even into the early years of television. At the time, few people questioned the deeper meanings behind the blackface anymore than one living today might question the deeper meanings behind those ghastly Japanese cartoons featuring giant robots that can turn into spaceships. Were a giant robot from outer space to see these cartoons, it might take quite a bit of offense at these stereotypes. Thank God this has yet to become an issue, because I, for one, don't know how we'd begin to deal with an angry giant space robot, short of nuclear war, which might very well destroy not only the giant space robot, but the entire human race. So you see, taken in context, minstrel shows were a necessary evil of the times.

Although Mother and Daddy will claim that they were married before I came into the picture, I have cleverly traced the math, and unless I was born six months premature, I was most certainly well on my way before the two young lovers performed their nuptials. Frankly, I don't know why they tried so hard to cover it up. Mother had little fear of rejection from the hobo community ... she had already deserted them anyway ... and Daddy grew up among so many whores, hopheads, and homos that an unwanted pregnancy must have seemed like a gift of warm figgy pudding to Granny and Granpapa-figgy being the most delicious of all puddings.

At the time of my birth, Doc Polka's show had moved on to Baltimore. Daddy was faced with a difficult decision: give up on his show business dreams and enter domestic life, or raise his child in the same environment in which he had been raised, with no home more permanent than a jism stain on a motel room comforter. Perhaps that's a poor analogy, those stains being quite impossible to remove. At any rate, he settled on settling, and, bidding Granny and Granpapa a fond *adieu*, he bought the house in Namsy Brooks where our story begins.

The place he did not buy was the place where our story actually begins, and that is the Stanley Theater in downtown Baltimore, which is where I was at the age of 5, watching the ceiling as the lights went down in the crowded auditorium.

As I said before, I had no more interest in the cinema than I did in astro-paleontology, having caught my grandparents' incredible Nip n' Tuck act when it had rolled into town some months prior, and walking away from it with the belief that the only pure art form involved blackening one's face with cork and acting like a negro in front of a live audience.

That is, until I heard the voice.

Five simple words, and my life was changed forever.

"You ain't heard nothin' yet," said Al Jolson on the silver screen, and my entire perception on the merits of film did a swift 180. Getting hit with shovels didn't much appeal to me, but talking on film in front of millions of people the world over struck me as a damn fine way to earn a dollar.

My future was decided. I was to become an actress.
And you ain't heard nothin' yet.

Chapter Two

A Star, Having Been Born Several Years Hence, Becomes a Star

Whereas before I would look for bugs in the juniper tree or beat rocks against other rocks in my spare time, acting now became my *raison d'être*. My first experience with acting in a formal setting was at 7 years old, in a local production of *Fifi the Kid*, a musical farce that was, to my generation, what *Annie* or *The Prancey Toads* would be to today's generation. Being a young theater aficionado, I had long considered the role of Fifi to be the pinnacle of theatrical success. Although I had never seen an actual production, I already had the book memorized, and I would spend hours singing along with the piano roll that Daddy had brought back to me from one of his trips to New York. When I heard that the Baltimore Fantasy Players would be performing the show, I knew I had to audition. Thankfully, Mother and Daddy were very encouraging of my thespian dreams, and they took me to the Western Palace Theater for the audition.

Although I belted my heart out that day, I was beat out for the lead role by another girl who went to my school. Her name was Rose Palmaroy, and she always wore cute little frilly pink dresses and her hair was always done up just so in precious little piggy-wiggy tails and all the boys thought she was the cat's meow and I loathed her. I was cast in the highly anonymous role of Little Girl #3.

Well, I wasn't going to stand for it. I knew Fifi's lines inside and out, and I wasn't about to let that nitwit Rose Palmaroy walk away with a role that was justifiably mine. Two days before dress rehearsal, while she was waiting for her mommy to come pick her up, Rose met with a little accident. Let's just say I pushed her down a flight of stairs.

With the lead actress out of the way, I convinced the director that I could play Fifi. The show opened to rave reviews in the *Baltimore Spectator*, *the Baltimore Sun*, and *Gay Times*-the weekly entertainment guide. Caustus Pfeiffer of the *Sun* said, "Little Karen Hitler's angelic performance as Fifi, the loveable ragamuffin, marks the promising debut of a future star of the Baltimore stage and, someday, perhaps even the cinema."

From the success of that early victory, I soon went on to recapture the magic time and again with starring roles in several Baltimore Fantasy shows, including *Someone's In the Kitchen, Good Ol' Mr. Porky*, and *The Flippinfloogle Follies*. I was blessed with an unusually easy transition into adolescence, and my beauty, voice, and acting abilities only improved with age.

Life at home was not so simple. The stock market crash in 1929 forced Daddy's employer to close the travel agency where he had been working since settling down in Namsy. I was too young at the time to recognize the profound effect this had on my family dynamics, but I do remember Daddy going through a long period of sleepless nights while trying to figure out how to keep our family afloat. Desperate for work, he invested his remaining savings in a trunk full of mops and headed out on the road. For the next few years, Daddy would be gone for months at a time, and Mother began to get restless. Domestic life was not all she had hoped it would be. She missed the freedom of the open rails, and she would get quite depressed at times, thinking about her old friends in the hobo community. She would spend hours sitting around the freight yard, waiting for old friends to pass by who could acquaint her with the latest goings-on with the train people.

Many years later, I found out the reason for Mother's restlessness, which I shall share with you now. This being a narrative, I could choose to withhold this information in order to make a more dramatic impact later down the line, but we still have plenty of surprises left, and, let's face it, you don't really care about Mother anymore than I did at this point. Unbeknownst to me for much of my life, Mother had been married to another man before Daddy. Not only that, but she had never gotten a proper divorce. My mother, I am sad to say, was a bigamist.

The truth was not revealed to me until later in life, over the course of a tearful reconciliation with my father. As the story goes, Slim Jim Pickford caught on to my mother's scent when she was just a fresh-faced 14 year-old, naïve to the dangerous ways of the hobo life. He took her under his wing and taught her the hobo code. Soon, they fell in love and got married in a traditional hobo ceremony.

Slim Jim was a hard-drinking man, and his fights with Mother were said to rock the boxcars damn near off the tracks. Mere days before she met my father in Tallapee, she left Slim Jim for good-or so she thought at the time. Try as she might, Mother couldn't shake the powerful grip that Slim Jim held over her heart. As the years went on, Mother became increasingly anxious to find her lost love.

In 1935, when I was 11 years old, she did just that.

By that time, Daddy had raised enough capital on the road to set up a small office in Namsy Brook. Starting in the spring of '34, Hitler's Cleaning Supplies finally kept him home for good, and with Mother having become a depressed alcoholic bitch, I was most grateful. Daddy recognized the change in her, and it did not sit well with him. Many were the nights he would come home from a hard day's work to find her passed out on the davenport, martini glass in one hand and a box of Fruity's Loops in the other, stinking of alcohol, sallow flesh begging for a conditioning lotion or, at the very least, a moist towelette. Shaking his head, he would go into the kitchen and get dinner ready for me when I came home from whatever dramatic piece I was starring in at the time.

It was during rehearsal for the Namsy Brooks Players' production of *Bobsy Goes A-Hunting* that I came home to find him sitting sadly at the kitchen table, a piece of notepaper in his hand.

"Daddy?" I asked, and he looked up at me with the shattered face of a man who has had his heart broken for the last time.

"She's gone," he said, and immediately I knew to whom he was referring. I had seen the wandering look in her eyes during those final days, and I knew she wasn't long for our family. According to her note, she hopped the 1:19 to Dubuque. 'Oh, Dubuque!' I remember thinking.

'How many women have you seduced with your wicked siren's call? And what have you planned for Mother, Dubuque? Where will she find herself on your wild streets?'

But Daddy knew what he was getting into. He knew he couldn't hold a fireball in his hand anymore than a tornado could be taught to Lindsey Hop. The irony didn't strike me until years later; my father, who waited at the train station for young girls of whom he could take advantage, had, himself, been taken advantage of by a woman who liked to ride on trains.

Chapter Three
Tragedy Continues to Strike

After Mother left, Daddy and I tried to pick up the shattered pieces of our lives by shutting the door on reality and locking away the key in a small, ivory box. We put ourselves on a strict film regiment that would impress even the staunchest video rental enthusiast of the modern age. During the weekday, we would hit the latest releases at least three nights a week. Weekends were reserved for matinees, and on the days when I didn't have rehearsals or performances, we caught an evening show as well. I wouldn't recommend our methods to everyone, but they suited Daddy and me just fine. Never did I feel more at home than when I was sitting in the balcony of the Stanley, watching my Hollywood idols dance, sing, fight, fall in love, fall out of love, and die over and over again. It seemed a perfect existence: getting paid to live the lives of others, while having a real life that was better than any role you could play.

And what a wonderful year for film it was! Charles Laughton in *Mutiny on the Bounty*. The hilarious Marx Brothers in *A Night at the Opera*. Alfred Hitchocock's *The 39 Steps*. Boris Karloff in *Bride of Frankenstein*. And my personal favorite, Bette Davis in *Dangerous*. Bette was everything I wanted to be ... loud, brash, self-confident, and beautiful. As the alcoholic Broadway has-been Joyce Heath, she blew everyone else off the screen and ended up clutching a little gold man named the Academy Award in her delicate hands later the next year.

While I fantasized about my future in the cinema, real life was raging outside. The Depression was coming to an end, but Daddy still had to fight tooth and nail for every new client he picked up. Granny and Granpapa, who had been struggling since the onset of the Depression, finally decided that the country no longer welcomed their Nip n' Tuck routine; that summer, they packed their traveling gear and used their savings to buy a precious little house in the Otterbein area of Baltimore, right next door to Namsy Brooks.

I was overjoyed to learn that Granny and Granpapa were moving so close to us. My grandparents were, to me, as famous and fascinating as any of my Hollywood idols. I did not know them as well as I would have liked to, as they were almost constantly on the road, and I was bound and determined to spend as much time with them as possible. The first night they came into town, Daddy and I cooked up a feast, and I sat at the dinner table in rapt attention as the three old showhands spun their tales of life on the road. Granny and Granpapa knew all of the great minstrel stars, like Mississippi Tan-Tan, "Dandy" Daddy Apples, and the Portly Kid. They had toured with Jane Romaine, eaten supper with Guy Frisco, and played golf with Buster Frogs and Cappy Harlot. Sadly, most of these names are lost to history. They were the stalwarts, the old-time performers, the nickel-and-dime dancers, singers, and showmen who had been rudely pushed out of the way by my beloved Hollywood.

Granny and Granpapa, for what it's worth, held no grudges. Even at the height of their fame, they could see the tide was turning for the American stage. They had made a comfortable career doing what they loved, and for that they had no complaints. Still relatively young by today's standards, they had their health, they had their family, and now they finally had the little house with the rose garden that Granny had dreamed of all her life.

"Oh, sure," Granny told me as she was leaving that night, "I have regrets. But you can't live on regrets, Karen. You can't eat regrets. If you're not careful, though, regrets just might eat you."

I have always cherished these words, both because they are very true, and because they were the last words Granny ever spoke to me.

The following day, as they were moving into their new home, Granpapa slipped off the balcony and fell into the little rose garden, sending rose petals flying into the spring air like so many lost dreams. Panicked, Granny ran out into the street to get help, only to be smashed head-on by a drunkard, fresh from the dealer in a brand new 1935 Chevrolet EA Master DeLuxe. Her body flew into the air, knocked into a low-hanging branch of the old oak tree on the front lawn, and collapsed on the ground in a grisly heap, only to be run over again by the thoroughly confused drunkard. She would never get the chance to smell those roses that had meant so very much to her.

Daddy saw the entire scene from down the road. He was driving to the house on his lunch break to surprise his parents with a carload of free cleaning products. Little did he know when he left the store that day that his products would be put to use immediately, cleaning blood and bits of Granny goo from the hard streets of Baltimore.

Granpapa was not killed in his fall, but he had been knocked into a vegetative state of limbo where the doctors predicted he would spend the rest of his days. Ever the optimist, Daddy reminded me that the two of them would have been useless without one another, and that it was best for both of them that they never had to see the other suffer. His words were little consolation. I couldn't help but imagine how awful that must have been for Daddy, watching his father and mother being slaughtered from afar and being powerless to stop it. I imagined this must be what it's like in one of those war-torn countries in Africa, where people brain each other with coconuts for a slice of pie.

It was on an overcast and drizzly day that we laid Granny to rest in St. Agnes's Municipal Cemetery. The theater community caught wind of Nip n' Tuck's sad final routine; all week long, Daddy and I had been opening cards and flowers from Granny and Granpapa's vaudeville friends. Many of the minstrel stars I had heard so much about flew in for the funeral, although it was difficult to recognize them when they were white.

After the funeral, Daddy and I hosted a party for the twenty or so people who had been kind enough to come into town. Reminiscing with his old friends and mentors did a lot to lift dad's spirits, and I saw him laugh for the first time since the accident. The stories that were told on that day have stuck with me forever, but I shall not share any of them with you. Some things, a girl has to keep for herself.

After a certain number of drinks had been drunk, the guests began begging Daddy for a little bit of the old Dignified Gentry routine. Daddy waved them off at first. The pleading grew louder. Finally, he relented. "But only," he said, "if my lovely daughter would do us the honor of performing the Tuck role."

Well, I have never been able to resist the demands of an audience that is begging to be entertained. Daddy and I launched into a flawless rendition of the famous routine, evoking peals of laughter from the group of forgotten celebrities. For my money, you can't beat the attention and appreciation you get from a funeral crowd.

After the routine, a man who kept to himself throughout the funeral and party pulled Daddy and me aside and handed us a card.

"Name's Jack Scallinger," he said, with a rapid-fire delivery that reminded me of a jackhammer wrapped in silk. "I was working with your folks on bringing their talents to the silver screen. If I may be blunt, that ain't gonna happen now. Their careers are over. But your daughter here, she's got something special. It would be a shame to waste her talents in this two-bit burg. I'm flying back to L.A. tonight, and when you're ready, you bring her on out and I'll make her a star. But don't wait too long," he said with a wink. "I don't want any of that beauty to go to waste."

Needless to say, I was overjoyed. Through their deaths, my grandparents had given me the best present an aspiring young actress could receive ... although Granpapa wasn't really dead, but lying supine in a hospital bed sucking Daddy's money down the drain with every life-supported beat of his heart. I'm no doctor, and I don't know the technical definition of death, but I think that's close enough.

Chapter Four
Hooray for Hollywood

We were both ready for a change, and so Daddy sold his store and the houses, shipped Granpapa off to an old folk's home, and drove us out to Los Angeles before the dirt had a chance to settle on Granny's grave. In a way, I think that all the tragedy of the past few months had been a wake-up call to Daddy-life was too short to waste struggling to become the next cleaning supplies tycoon. Despite his wife leaving him, his mother dying, and his father turning into a vegetable-in-man-clothing, he still carried that infectious optimism that kept us both going through trying times. We didn't know what awaited us out in California, but as Daddy always said, "When the chips are down, try the pretzels."

I vividly recall the moment when we drove into town to see the enormous letters spread out across the mountain-HOLLYWOODLAND.

"You see that, baby?" my daddy asked. "That's where we're going to be living someday. High up there in the hills, right next door to Douglas Fairbanks and Mary Pickford."

For the time being, however, we kept driving-all the way to the Tuckered Trucker Motor Lodge in Burbank, where we would spend our first, tenuous month in California.

The first order of business was to enroll me in school. While I was sad to leave my friends behind in Baltimore, I was not that sad, because I didn't really have any friends. My friends were a transient, ever-changing group, actors and actresses all, collected over the course of one show and tossed to the side when the next dramatic piece came around. When I was younger, I prided myself on my older friends, thinking myself more worldly and learned than the mumbling child-beasts in my age group. Now that I'm not so young, I feel as though I may have been mistaken in my rush to grow up. While other children my age were playing kick the can and fatty-in-the-corner, I was cozying up to perverse older men who secretly longed to get their shaking hands on my tight young flesh. While other children were blowing on pinwheels and giving each other the heebie-jeebies with scare masks, I was flouncing around in hoop skirts, pretending to be a lady of the Renaissance, often times on stage.

I was anxious for the fresh start that living in Los Angeles would give me. I imagined the Hollywood kids would be a breed apart from the lollipop-slurping twidgets I knew back home. Back in Baltimore, the kids thought of me as an outsider, a loner. Here in Hollywood, among the children of moguls and aspiring thespians, I fancied I would finally find my place.

But it was not to be. Daddy and I were turned away at the door of the school. "Where are your transcripts?" the aging lizard behind the desk asked us.

"Transcripts?" we replied, unwise to the lingo of the Los Angeles school system.

"You can't enroll without transcripts."

Discouraged, we returned to the motor lodge and called my old school. Namsy Brooks, we learned, only had enough money to keep updated transcripts for the students who distinguished themselves through academic achievement. I was no knucklehead, but I was hardly at the top of my class. As a result, there was no paper trail for my life. I was, as we say in the biz, a free agent.

We returned to the school and pleaded our case, but the administration stood strong. "You must realize, Mr. and Miss Hitler, we are already well over our quota of students. In the last three years, our student population has nearly doubled. We simply cannot afford to take a chance on a child with no past."

That was the last time I ever set foot inside an academic institution. If you ask me, learning is overrated, anyway. Did Alexander the Great have to memorize his multiplication tables? Could Marie Antoinette diagram a sentence? All the books in the world can't substitute for the greatest teacher of them all: life. Except, perhaps, this book. And *Tuesdays with Morrie*. I quite enjoyed that.

Now that I was officially a school system reject, the next order of business was my career. We put in a call to Jack Scallinger and spoke with his secretary, who told us that Mr. Scallinger would be out of town for two weeks, but she would have him call us as soon as he returned. So far, our new life was not quite turning out the way we had planned.

Then there was the small business of a weekly income. With my hopes of breadwinning put on hold for another few weeks, Daddy hit the streets to look for a job. Every day, he left the hotel in the early morning and drove around, searching for a kind employer who would take in a man with a history of smart business practices. As far as money went, we were in better shape than many at the time, but money can go quickly when you have a growing daughter and a hospitalized father to support. These days were among the longest of my life. Lacking the skills to drive a car and a car to drive them with, I spent my days alone at the Tuckered Trucker, bored out of my mind. All around me, the film capital of the world jounced and bustled with the promise of celebrity, and there I was, stuck in a motel room in Burbank, with little more than a cat's cradle string to entertain me. Burbank hasn't changed much since those days, save for the erection of a few powerful studios. Smog was not yet a problem, of course, but it was just as muggy and disgusting as it is today.

Charming and intelligent as he was, it was not long before Daddy found employment as a manager at a hardware store. Daddy was cheered by the sudden stroke of good fortune, and he took me out to the world-famous Musso & Frank Grill to celebrate. I was ecstatic. Although Musso & Frank was no longer the hottest of the hot spots in Hollywood, Tom Cherry and Margaret Donovan had been photographed there in the recent issue of *Photoplay*, and I was certain that this evening would hold promise for a star-struck kid from Baltimore; that is, me.

How right I was. The minute we walked in, I sensed the presence of greatness. It's an odd feeling, I will admit, but one that I have felt many times since. Some stars are just that-stars, with their very own gravitational pull that you can feel when you encounter them. It was like a great tornado was spiraling through Musso & Frank, sucking up the plebeians into the swirling vortex of fame at the center. I tugged on Daddy's sleeve.

"Do you feel that, Daddy?" I asked. "Someone is here."

Daddy smiled and rolled his eyes. Although he enjoyed going to the pictures and he was very supportive of my Hollywood dreams, he still had a hard time shaking the thought that it was all just a novelty; that the stage would win out in the end. He could not sense the pull of Hollywood as I could.

I understand perfectly; everyone is tuned into his own cultural wavelength. You could sit Joe DiMaggio or Mickey Mattingly in front of me and I wouldn't give a hoot. "Oh, throw a ball around for a living, do you?" I would ask. "Sounds fascinating." I would say this part sarcastically. Likewise, an Eskimo might be drawn toward the world's most famous whale-killer or what have you, while I would be far more intrigued by one of those delightful little snow seals.

We were seated at our table, and the silverware practically leapt from the tablecloth in the direction of the W.C. I told Daddy that I must freshen up for dinner, and, like a spaceman under control of a devious zombie-ray, I headed toward the force.

Seated at an inconspicuous booth just outside the W.C., cloaked in darkness, was my idol: none other than Miss Bette Davis, herself.

My heart did a double take. I went into the W.C. and stared at myself in the looking glass. 'Calm yourself, Karen,' I thought. 'Bette Davis will soon be hoping that you will talk to her as she passes your table.' Strength gathered thusly, I washed my hands and left the W.C. to face my destiny head-on.

"Miss Davis," I said.

The other patrons at the table gasped. Bette's no-nonsense reputation was well known at the time, and I'm sure most people would not have had the courage to approach her as I did. But I was not most people-I was Karen Hitler, future superstar of the highest order. Bette could sense something in me, I could tell. She stared at me with that impenetrable gaze that has been so well utilized in dozens of pictures over the years. She looked me up and down, cigarette smoke billowing out of her delicate hands and circling through the air like a pack of guard dogs. I decided immediately that I must take up smoking.

Finally, she spoke. In her dry, accented warble, she asked, "How may I help you, dear?"

"You're my favorite actress, Miss Davis," I said, my pulse pounding my earlobes into a twittery Jell-O. "I just know you're going to win the Academy Award this year, I just know it."

"Thank you, dear," she replied, nodding.

The man across the table from her began to rise, ready to shoo me away. But I was not going to be ignored. I had made it this far, and I wasn't leaving until I let Miss Davis know just exactly who I was. Bette, sensing that I meant business, shot the man a glare. He sat back down.

"I don't want to bother you in the middle of your dinner, Miss Davis, so I'll just ask one question and I will be on my way."

"Fine," Bette assented.

"I'm an actress, Miss Davis. And I'm good. I'm darn good. And I just want to know if you have any advice for someone who would one day like to act in the pictures with you."

Bette smiled.

"Try the chowder, darling," she said. "It's simply divine."

To many, this might have seemed a silly joke, meant to put an end to an obnoxious conversation. But I knew Bette better than that. She simply didn't make silly jokes at the expense of others. If Bette Davis didn't like you, she would tell it to you straight. Contained in her advice were pearls of wisdom. I didn't have time to figure them out at the moment, but I knew that if I looked deeply enough, I would find everything I needed to know inside her words. You see, I was observant. I looked down at her meal and noticed that *she wasn't eating chowder.* The man across from her stifled a laugh. He was a buffoon. He had no business dining with the finest actress, nay, the finest woman on the planet. I nodded to Bette, who nodded back.

"Thank you, Miss Davis," I said. "I will always cherish your words."

"Fine, darling," she replied. "Fine."

I didn't tell Daddy what happened when I got back to the table. My conversation with Bette would remain my personal little secret. Daddy would have just done something silly, anyway, like gone over to her table and asked for an autograph. This one was all mine.

For dinner, I requested the chowder. Turns out, it wasn't even on the menu.

Chapter Five
An Agent Is Enlisted

Daddy got to work selling widgets and sprinkle systems at the hardware store, and I got to work sitting on my rump around the pool at the Tuckered Trucker. Every afternoon, I would place a call to Mr. Scallinger's office, then go down to the pool and dip my toes in the water while reading about the glamorous lives of celebrities in *Photoplay* and *Vanity Fair*. It was torture, knowing I was so close to all of the glamorous places described in the magazines, yet here I was, stuck in the lowest-rent dive in the Valley. I imagine darling little Moonie Zappa must have had similar feelings when she was working on that novelty hit that catapulted the girls of the Valley into the spotlight a few years back. "Poor me," Moonie probably said to herself, "how will I ever become famous? I have no access to celebrity to speak of, yet I have this song here that might turn a head or two." I say, good for her. I applaud anyone who can stretch her abilities and means to the breaking point and find her way into the national spotlight.

I did not have quite as much luck as dear Moonie. My depression grew ever stronger as I leafed through the magazines. Pictured here was Joan Crawford with her agent on the set of *Girls Can't Lie;* over there, Ross Alexander laughing it up at Twenty-One with his agent; still further over there, on the next page, was Mae West and her agent, celebrating the release of *The Giant Jewess*. The signs were everywhere;

if I ever hoped to succeed, I needed a Svengali. The only connection we had was Jack Scallinger, who seemed to be out of touch. I had little hope that someone was going to discover me wading in the pool at the Tuckered Trucker, although I did have my fantasies.

"Enough is enough," I finally told Daddy, after a third week of feeling completely unaccomplished. "I cannot sit around this place for one more day. You must take me to Jack Scallinger's office immediately. If he is not at his office, we will find out where he lives."

Daddy, I think, had been so caught up in the exciting new world of hardware that he hadn't even noticed my suffering. Well, he was noticing now, all right.

"Of course," Daddy said. "I'll get my hat."

We got into the car and drove out to Jack's office in Santa Monica. Daddy waited in the car while I knocked on the door. No answer. I knocked again. Still no answer. I looked back at Daddy, who shut the car off and met me on the steps. He pounded on the door.

"All right, Scallinger, we know you're in there! Answer this door right now or I'm breaking it down!"

Daddy could be quite forceful when he wanted to be.

The door opened a crack, and Jack timidly stuck his head up to the opening. When he saw Daddy and me standing there, he opened the door up wider.

"Can I help you?" he asked, worriedly.

"Damn right you can help us," Daddy said. "My little girl here has been calling you for three weeks, trying to make an appointment. Back in Baltimore, you told us that if we could get out here, you could make her a star. Well, we're here. Now get to work."

A light of recognition traveled across Scallinger's face.

"Oh, yes!" he exclaimed, "I remember you! The girl with the marvelous voice! Smashing! Oh, do come in!"

He opened the door all the way and ushered us into his small, cramped office. Besides his desk and chair, the only item of furniture in the office was a small cot in the corner, covered with clothing and papers. I shot Daddy a nervous glance. This was not what I imagined a Hollywood agent's office would look like.

He motioned us to sit down on the cot. We cleared off a spot and settled onto the filthy, rickety mattress.

"Now, remind me of your name," he snapped, with machine gun quickness. "It's the same as some world leader, yes? Mussolini? No. Roosevelt? No, that's not right. I'm not quite getting it. Help me out here. Come on, chop, chop."

"Hitler," Daddy and I blurted together.

"Ah, yes, Hitler, the Kraut. Don't have anything against the Germans myself, a fine people. Didn't do so hot in the big war, but what're ya' gonna do? All right, Hitler, then. First things first, we're gonna have to change that. I don't know Adolph Hitler from Little Miss Muffet, but I do know that no one's gonna like ya' if you've got the last name of a tyrant. What's your first name again?"

"Karen," I answered.

"And middle?"

"Jameson."

"Karen Jameson. Nope, don't like it. Karen James... Karen Mason... Ah-ha!" he shouted, holding his hands in the air and pantomiming a marquee shape. "Karen Jamey."

I looked at Daddy, who was still sizing up the situation.

"Uh, all right," I said.

"Atta girl!" Jack exploded. "Ya' got yourself a smart little girl here, Pops," he said to Daddy. "But I'm gonna make her smarter."

Having been raised in the world of performers, Daddy had an instant mistrust of anyone he met, and Jack Scallinger was as slick as a greased baboon. I could tell Daddy was keeping his mouth shut for my sake, but on this last comment, he exploded.

"Now look here, Scallinger," he said. "I don't know what your angle is, but this is all moving a little too fast for my taste. We've been here two minutes and you've already got her changing her name. I don't know much about how you Hollywood types operate, but I'm willing to bet that Myron Selznick doesn't have to sleep in his office. Now, we're looking to you for help, because we don't know anyone, and my little girl here is damn talented. Why don't you tell me what you can do for us?"

A smile crept over Scallinger's lips. He leaned forward in his chair and put his elbows on the table.

"All right, chum, I can see you're a smart man, and pardon my French, but you're not the kind of guy who falls for a line of bullshit. I respect that. First things first-I'm staying in my office because my wife just kicked me out. I don't want to get into details, but let's just say it's all her fault. As for part two, I know it may look bad from that side of the desk, but I've got a lot of opportunities just piling up in here and I've been waiting for the right actress to share them with. I think that actress just might be your little girl."

"What kind of opportunities?" I interrupted.

"Well, let's see now," Jack began, leaning back in his chair. "Got the inside scoop on the new Katherine Hepburn picture. They're looking for a girl to play her sister. Think you might be the perfect candidate."

Daddy started to speak, but I cut him off. "When's the audition and what do I have to wear?"

Scallinger tilted further back and let out a laugh.

"She's a whip, ain't she, Pops?" he asked.

"Call me Jebediah," Daddy said, icily.

"Well, look," Jack said, "before I can send you out on auditions, you're gonna have to sign a contract. It's a cutthroat business, babe. Little honey of a peach like you gets in front of the camera without an agent, and they're gonna yank you right out from under me."

"Where's the contract?" I asked.

"Now hold on a minute, Scallinger," Daddy said. "My daughter isn't signing anything until we find out the terms."

"Of course, of course," Jack agreed. "Hey, look, I'm not trying to pull a fast one on you, Jeb. I know what your little girl's worth in the marketplace, and I just wanna make sure we get a fair price. Trust me, you'll thank me when you see her pretty little face smiling back at you in the pages of *Variety*."

"All right, Scallinger," Daddy finally relented. "We'll take a look at the contract. But we're not signing anything until we know exactly what we're signing."

"A wise man, a wise man," Jack said, with a note of reverence in his voice.

"So, where's the contract?" Daddy asked.

"You're sitting on it," Scallinger replied.

Back at the Tuckered Trucker, Daddy and I went through the terms of the contract. Most of it was legal mumbo-jumbo that I couldn't understand. Daddy had a little more knowledge, having owned his own business for a spell, but we were both clueless when it came to the standard terms of an acting contract. Daddy's main concern was making sure that I got my fair share of the profits. According to the contract, Scallinger was entitled to 30% of my earnings. This seemed a bit high to Daddy. "I'm not going higher than 25," he said. Of course, it didn't take me long after I signed the contract to discover that 10% was standard, but at the time, I didn't care. Whatever it took to get me on that audition was okay by me.

Daddy had the next day off, so we went back to Jack's office to haggle over the fine points. This time Jack was prepared. The cot was packed up, the clothes and papers were out of sight, and the office actually looked somewhat presentable. Oddly, although we had spoken with his secretary the first time we called, I saw no secretary in the office, nor did I see a place to put one, were she there. Another strange little difference was that the walls, which were bare the day before, were now covered with signed headshots of actors and actresses.

"Are these the people you represent, Mr. Scallinger?" I asked.

"Yep, yep, that's them," he nodded.

"You represent Clark Gable?" I asked, excitedly.

"Well, all of them, except that one," he answered.

"Queenie Thompson?"

"Almost," he answered. "Green card problem."

I left the conversation at that. Daddy was raring to crack into the contract. As I had little interest in hearing them quibble, I slipped on my sunglasses and went outside to wander the streets a bit. Although Santa Monica was, at that time, already a central hub of Hollywood activity, Jack Scallinger's office was not in the sort of area that could be referred to as either "central" or a "hub." Shady characters darted in and out of the shadows that fell from the buildings next to Jack's office. Shady characters, it seems, can always find a shadow when they need one.

As I stood in front of the office, blowing Double Bubbles and trying to find a direction in which to move, one of these shady characters approached me with a shuffling strut that I would come to know all too well in the subsequent years. Having lived my entire life in Namsy Brooks, I didn't quite know how to respond to the approach of a menacing stranger. I froze in place, hoping to God that I would make it out of the conversation alive.

"Hey there, little lady," the man said in a stiff New York accent.

"Hey there, yourself," I replied.

I popped an enormous pink bubble and sucked it back in one quick breath. The man moved closer. I recognize now that I was playing with fire, flirting with an obvious degenerate, but at the time I thought I was the queen of the world. My only interaction with older men had been with the perverts and has-beens acting in the Baltimore theater community. I knew the effect I had on them, and I considered it a special power that must be utilized as much as possible. I don't recommend it for all 13-year-old girls, especially with all those killers and pedophiles walking around in the Internets and such.

The degenerate leaned against the wall next to me and lit up a cigarette. His stocky belly heaved as he sucked in the pleasurable mentholated smoke. I gobbled my Double Bubble in what I thought to be a coy manner.

"Name's Tony Tarantella," he said, eyeing me from behind his sunglasses. "Don't recall seeing you around here before."

"I'm signing a contract with my agent."

"Oh yeah?" he asked, raising a smooth eyebrow. "You an actress?"

"Yeah," I said. "What's it to you?"

Tony Tarantella smiled, revealing a dazzling set of pearly white teeth.

"You're feisty, little girl," he said.

"Feisty like a fox," I answered. This guy was starting to give me the creeps. I chewed my gum nervously and inched toward the doorway. "Anyhow, I gotta go inside and see what my Daddy is doing. It was nice meeting you, Mr. Tarantella."

He stared at me with a half-cocked grin, both eyebrows in firing position. "You call me Tony, little girl," he said, deliberately. "I'll be seeing you again soon."

I twisted the doorknob and scurried inside to see Daddy and Jack in the midst of a firm handshake. At the sound of the door, they turned to me and smiled wide, hands still clasped firmly above the cheap wooden desk.

"Question for ya', Karen Jamey," Jack smirked. "Are ya' ready for your close-up?"

Chapter Six

An Auspicious Beginning

Daddy felt like a million bucks, having bargained Jack Scallinger all the way down to 20%. Jack took us out to the Italian restaurant around the block to celebrate. When we arrived, who should be standing in a tuxedo at the maitre-de's station but my close, new friend Tony Tarantella? I was relieved to see he wasn't the degenerate I thought him to be. I would learn one day in the future that he was every bit so and more. Truth be told, I had experienced a rather strange sensation when I met Tony, as though our paths were destined to cross again in this vast plain of existence known as life. You see, I have always had a sort of sixth sense, or precognition, as the experts would say. For instance, just the other day, my roommate Myrna was going on and on about a lost hairclip. "Where's my hairclip, where's my hairclip?" she kept asking, like a skipping recording of skipping records. Finally, when I could no longer bear to hear her inane gibber any longer, a flash came into my head of the bottom of the radiator. For a brief spell, I actually became the hairclip in question. "I'm under here," I said in a high-pitched squeaky voice. "What's that?" Myrna asked. I snapped back into reality. "Under the radiator," I said. And lo and behold, where was that damned hairclip? Right under the radiator.

"We meet again," Tony said to me, seductively. In place of his sunglasses was a pair of devastating blue-gray eyes. The world around us became an ice cream swirl as he reached into my head and massaged my brain with his pupils. He was a big man, but not unfit, and in the tuxedo he held a degree of gravitas that I had not detected in our earlier conversation.

"Jebediah Hitler," Daddy interrupted, waking me from my reverie. "We'll take a table for three, garçon."

Daddy fixed his coolest gaze upon the hulking maitre-de, who stared back in kind. Each waited for the other to break while Jack Scallinger fretted nervously in the background. The tension was unbearable, until finally, Jack spoke up.

"Uh, Mr. Tarantella, my friend here meant no disrespect," Jack said.

"Of course he didn't," Tony said slowly, his lips breaking into a combination snarl and smile ... a smarl, if you will. "You are here to celebrate, and you shall have the best table in this house. Your little girl," he said, looking at Daddy, "deserves nothing but the best."

Tony whistled and a waiter in a slightly shabbier tuxedo bounded up to greet us.

"Seat them in the Blue Room," Tony said.

The waiter smiled widely. "Yes sir, Mr. Tarantella. Nothing but the best for friends of Mr. Tarantella. Right this way, please."

Daddy nodded coolly to Tony, then followed the waiter back through the restaurant. As I walked by him, Tony whispered, "I told you I'd see you again." I looked at him and smiled, and his face softened. I could tell that underneath the gruff exterior beat the heart of a gentleman- a degenerate gentleman, but a gentleman, nonetheless.

The Blue Room was as lavish and blue as the name would suggest. We were seated at a private booth in the far back corner. At the front of the room, a torch singer in a sleek velvet dress ran through Italian classics. I could get used to this kind of treatment.

"All right," Jack whispered to me, as soon as the waiter left. "How do you know Tony Tarantella?"

"The man in the monkey suit?" I asked.

Jack shushed me. "Keep your voice down," he said.

"He introduced himself to me outside of your office," I answered.

"I don't like the way he looked at my daughter," Daddy said, in a huff.

"Yeah, well, suck it up, Jeb," Jack replied. "Tony Tarantella is only the most powerful gangster in West L.A. You should be happy he's just looking. Guy like that could snap her out from under you and there wouldn't be nothin' you could do about it, 'lest you wanted to wake up six feet under the ground."

At that, my pulse raced. Here I was, only three weeks into my tenure in Los Angeles, and already I was associating with known gangsters. The thought of it gave me the shivers in a good way.

"The most powerful gangster in West L.A. is a maitre-de?" Daddy asked, skeptical.

"That ain't no maitre-de, Buster. Tony Tarantella owns this place, along with most of the police force, the mayor, and a handful of Chinese laundromats. Trust me, Baltimore, there are certain people you don't want to mess with out here, and Tony Tarantella is several of those people. You thank your lucky stars he's taken a shine to your daughter and leave it at that."

"Well, I still don't care for it," Daddy answered.

"Put it out of your mind, Jeb," Jack said. "We got business to discuss."

Daddy grumbled and stared at his menu.

Over the course of dinner, Jack told me about his plans for my career, and I will admit, they were exciting. First thing the next morning, he would arrange a screen test through an acquaintance at Republic pictures, a brand new, independent production company that mostly made crime pictures and cowboy films. "None of the major studios will look at a nobody unless she has a screen test," Jack assured us. "But that's an easy problem to fix. Once we get the reel developed, I have a friend over at RKO who can get it on the desk of David Sarnoff. From there, the role is in the bag. One look at you, kiddo, and they won't even bother looking at anyone else."

The plan sounded simple enough, and, true to his word, Jack called me out to the newly built Republic studios for my first screen test in the morning. Although Daddy had to work, he left me enough money to take a cab to the studio so that I wouldn't be late. The night before, we ran through a few performance pieces for the test: scraps of various songs and scenes I'd done in Baltimore productions, as well as a classic solo Tuck moment from Granny and Granpapa's hilarious "Caged Chicken" routine. Daddy helped me apply my cork before he left for work.

Dressed in my Sunday finest, I wandered out into the streets of Burbank to hail a cab. For several minutes, empty cars whizzed by, their drivers turning a blind eye to my needs. When I finally realized why they were bypassing me, it gave me a lesson in tolerance that I still hold dear to this day. Well, I was a girl on a mission, and I was not about to let racial prejudice deter me from my all-important screen test. The next taxicab that came along, I ran into the street in front of it. Waving my money in the air, I hopped up and down shouting, "I'm not a Negro! I'm not a Negro!" The cab came to a screeching halt in front of me, and the first hurdle was surpassed.

Much like Jack Scallinger's office, the Republic Pictures studios were not what I imagined Hollywood studios would look like. Where I expected to see a sprawling network of buildings around which mingled soldiers, chorus girls, and the like, I found instead a single, ugly, gray warehouse in the middle of nowheresville. I did not have to deal with the fearsome security guard at the gate because there was no gate, just a lonely, handmade sign at the end of a dirt road marking the studio's entrance.

I gathered my petticoats in my hands and trundled up the dirt walkway to the door. Jack stood outside, smoking a cigarette. When he saw me, his eyes practically leaped out of his head.

"Oh, no, no, no, no," he tsked, "whaddya think, you're trying out for *Birth of a Nation*? Ya' gotta get this cork off your face immediately."

Remember, I was only 13, and, as grown-up as I liked to consider myself, I had not yet developed the hard outer shell that is required in the cold, uncaring world of Hollywood. The look of shock on Jack's face told me that I had made a major faux pas by showing up at the audition in blackface. I burst into tears. Tears mingled with cork, smearing my makeup into the collar of my Sunday finery. Fifteen minutes before my first screen test, and I was a miserable wreck.

"Hey, hey," Jack said, softly. "Don't cry, little lady. We'll get ya' cleaned up good as new. Once these bastards see your pretty face, they're gonna flip!"

"Yeah?" I sniffled.

"I'm sure of it, doll face," he answered. "Now let's go get you cleaned up."

As soon as we walked in the door, the staid outer veneer of Republic Pictures was torn asunder. Figuratively, of course. At the front of the enormous building, secretaries scurried back and forth between an island of ringing telephones and clacking typewriters. Beyond this "office" area, dozens of Negroes roamed willy-nilly, while a white man in riding clothes barked orders through a conical megaphone. Jack scanned the room for the nearest water closet. Suddenly, the man in the riding clothes threw his megaphone down and stormed into the offices.

"I can't work this way, do you hear me?" he shouted to no one in particular.

His eyes landed on me.

"What the fuck are you doing back here?" he screamed. "Get on the fucking set!"

Thankfully, Jack intercepted.

"She's just here for a screen test," he said.

"We don't have time for a screen test!" the man exploded. "Can she act?"

"Yes sir," I answered.

"Then you're in the picture," he said to me. "Straighten up that makeup and get on the set in five minutes."

Unbeknownst to many of my biggest fanatics, that day marked my big screen debut. I was paid $20 for one line and one day's work on the set of the race picture *Hot Money!* I was Daphne, daughter of the mayor of a fantastical Southern town that was populated only by Negroes. The extras were all real Negroes, while the starring roles were played by whites in blackface, as was the custom at the time. My first line ever spoken on film was a tearful, "Ith Mama gwan die?" I nailed it on the first take and walked out of the studio $16 richer, after Jack took his cut.

Jack was positively ecstatic about this fortunate turn of events. I have a feeling that $4 was more money than he'd earned in quite some time. He was so happy that I didn't have the heart to remind him we never had a chance to shoot my screen test. Sometimes I think if we had, my life would have been immeasurably different. But as Granny said, one mustn't have regrets. The only way to change your past is to find everyone who interacted with you during that time and subject them to some sort of memory-altering procedure, and I'm pretty sure that the U.S. military are the only people who would have the techno- logical know-how to pull off that kind of thing.

When I returned home and told Daddy about my day, he beamed like a plump Thanksgiving clam. I told him the picture would only be seen by black audiences, but he didn't care. A screen credit was a screen credit, as far as Daddy was concerned. Me, I wasn't so sure. Don't get me wrong-it was nice to have that $16 in my pocket, but play- ing Daphne in *Hot Money!* wasn't my idea of taking Hollywood by storm.

The next morning, I got a call from Jack that would change my life forever. Apparently, a producer named Col Weissberger had seen the dailies of my performance and declared me the perfect actress to play the role of Lil' Suzy in a traveling production he was casting called *The New Soul Revue.* "Can ya' imagine, Karen?" he asked. "And to think that you were considering taking off the blackface. Weissberger is one of the biggest Vaudeville producers in the country! A gig like this is going to send your stock soaring!"

I was hesitant. First of all, much as I loved Granny and Granpapa's minstrel work, I did not look forward to spending the next four months pretending to be a member of another race. Second of all, my experi- ence with the taxicab and on the set of *Hot Money!* had left me with a strange feeling about the whole nature of minstrelsy. I couldn't quite see the fairness in having white people play black people when there were plenty of perfectly competent black actors and actresses walking around. Third of all, I didn't much care to take off from Hollywood just when things were starting to go my way.

Surprisingly, when I talked to Daddy about it that night, he was all for the idea. "Baby, there's nothing like the road to get you going," he said. "After you get done with this tour, you'll be poised for greatness. Much as I'm going to miss you, if you really want to make this crazy dream work, you can't let opportunities like this pass you by."

One week later, I boarded a bus with a thirty-piece cast and crew and hit the road-the road to adventure, the road to stardom, and, most importantly, the road to the theaters where the shows were to be performed.

Chapter Seven

Tourism

It didn't take me long to discover that *The New Soul Revue* was not the fantastic opportunity that everyone had promised. When one hears the words "tour bus," one thinks of a luxury hotel on wheels, complete with sleeping quarters, changing rooms, a davenport, and unlimited snacks of the finest brand quality. Our tour bus had none of these things. It was just a bus. The seats weren't even cushioned. Although we had reservations at hotel rooms in all of our major destinations, the majority of our time was to be spent traveling from place to place in this hulking, uncomfortable death trap.

As soon as we hit the road, we got to work. The director was a bald-headed German man named Pinky Strudels, and he approached the cast of his minstrel show like a slave driver approaches his slaves-in a very frightening manner, and often from behind. After going through a quick round of introductions, he handed out the script and began rehearsals immediately. Rehearsing a Broadway-size production in a three-foot wide aisle is not my idea of quality prep work, especially when the entire back third of the bus is taken up by props and sets.

At the very least, my part was substantial. *The New Soul Revue* told the story of the Soul family, a singing and dancing family of singers and dancers who sang and danced their way through comical situations and cliff-hanging adventures. I played Lil' Suzy Soul, the middle daughter. Real-life sisters Samantha and Rose Farquhar played my sisters, Teeny and Bertha Soul, respectively. Our two older brothers, Smokey and Pokey Soul, were played by Petey Nickles and Shermie Hempstead, again, respectively. Margaret Postelthwaite was the matriarch of the family, Jemima Soul. And as my father, Big Smokey, the one person in the cast who had any sort of name recognition: Fletcher Bisque.

Fletcher Bisque was one of the many silent film stars who fell on hard times when talkies came to prominence. He had a fine speaking voice, and his acting skills were above par, but his propensity for drink and sex with underage girls made him too much of a liability for the major studios who could find a million dashing young men to take his place. So Fletcher, who had no skills beyond his ability to entertain a crowd, was forced to sign up for excruciating tours such as *The New Soul Revue* for a pittance of what he would earn in one day of film acting.

As Lil' Suzy, I got to perform the big show-stopping number, "Stick a Lil' Plum In It." The song had been a hit a few years back as recorded by Martin Ivey, and I like to think that my rendition could have been a hit, as well, had we gotten the money together to do a cast recording. Unfortunately, Col Weissberger, as I learned, was not only a legendary producer, but a notorious cheapskate. Aside from the shoddy tour bus and rehearsal conditions, we were only allowed two meals a day, which usually consisted of eggs and beans. These two foodstuffs are a potent combination, and the atmosphere in the tour bus was hardly pleasant after 30 people had eaten their fill. Because it smelled like farts, you see.

Our first stop on the tour was the Ormsby County Fair in Carson City, Nevada. A mere two days after leaving Los Angeles and with no practice on an actual stage, we performed the entire hour-long musical for an unappreciative crowd of about twelve festival attendees. To be fair, we were competing with the wild hog races, which, given the choice, I would have certainly rather seen myself. As custom dictated, Pinky gave us the post-show notes and psychological abuse, then sent us back to our hotel for our first night's sleep in a real bed.

Here again, Col Weissberger didn't miss a chance to save a buck, forcing Samantha and Rose Farquhar and I to sleep together in a single twin-sized bed. For whatever reason, the sisters had taken an instant dislike to me. All attempts at friendly chatter over the previous two days had been met with stone-cold silence from the two evil she-beasts. As soon as we closed the door to our room, they turned to me and said, in unison, "We're gonna fucking kill you," then broke into demonic laughter that chilled me to the very bone.

I have always had the difficult gift of knowing when I am not wanted. Some people are lucky enough to live in blissful ignorance of the thoughts of those around them, but not me. Take my roommate Myrna, for example. I can't tell you how many times she's prattled on to me about that toothless idiot down the hall who she thinks is in love with her. "Joe Smoley is gonna be mah husband someday," she says. "He better hurry up," I tell her, "or you'll be spending your honeymoon in a casket." And still on she prattles, oblivious to the mean-spirited hatred behind my quips.

Now, usually when I am treated unfairly, I immediately get to work developing a plan for revenge. At this point, however, the pressure of my first tour compounded with the ill treatment by the Farquhar sisters simply overwhelmed me. I calmly stepped out of the room, walked a few paces down the hallway, and burst into tears.

A door next to me opened and out came Fletcher Bisque, dressed in a nightgown. Upon spotting the source of the hallway whimpering, he rushed over and embraced me.

"Whatever is the matter, little Karen?" he asked.

His strong arms felt good around my body, protective. I squeezed him tight and sobbed into his chest.

"They're horrible, horrible," I sniffled. "I wish I'd never come on this stupid, stupid tour."

"It's pretty much the pits all right," Fletcher agreed. "I think you could use a little drink."

"O-okay," I squeaked through my tears.

Fletcher led me into his room. Being the star of the show, he was the only one who got his very own room. It still wasn't the lap of luxury, but it was a good sight better than having to squeeze into a twin bed with two shrieking harpies.

He uncorked a bottle of whiskey and poured us each two heaping glasses. Having come of age in the Prohibition era, I had never taken even a sip of alcohol before. I did not want to appear to be a little girl in front of the famous Fletcher Bisque, though, so I accepted the glass and the toast that went with it. I still remember that first sip. Many people have a negative experience the first time they take a drink, alcohol being a rather acquired taste. I must have somehow acquired the taste in the womb, for that first drink went down smooth as cotton candy. Fletcher had already downed his glass and was pouring himself a second.

"You know, Karen," he said. "I envy you, I really do. You have your whole future ahead of you. Me, I'm washed up at age forty, a has-been. This is what I have to look forward to for the rest of my life-playing for rubes in between pie-eating contests and cattle roping demonstrations. I know it may seem tough now, but we'll get through it together, you and me. I like you, Karen. I knew from the first minute I saw you that you had something special."

"You did?" I asked, every bit the wide-eyed youngster. But I was no fool. I knew Fletcher's type all too well, having learned to fend for myself in my years on the Baltimore stages. Still, there was something noble about Fletcher Bisque that shone through his depressed exterior. He *had* been a movie star, after all. I had the feeling that if I played my cards right, I just might use this situation to my advantage.

We stayed up late into the night, drinking whiskey and laughing about the miserable conditions we had to endure. I was happy to have someone to talk to, and Fletcher was an excellent conversationalist. He told me stories about the old days in Hollywood, when acting consisted mainly of gesticulating wildly in front of a primitive camera, while the director shouted notes from across the room. To his credit, Fletcher was a complete gentleman. He did not put the moves on me. I slept with him anyway.

It was both the most painful and the most exhilarating experience of my life. Fletcher treated me quite gently, although, no matter how gentle one may be, a penis ramming into your vagina for the first time is no walk in the park, especially when the parties involved are either hung like a horse or thirteen. I know I have played myself up as a naïve youngster in this narrative, but I was wiser than I let on. Even at that young age, I understood perfectly well the power that sexual ability would bring me, and I had been itching to meet the man who would be bold enough to take my virginity and pitch it into the wastebasket of time. Fletcher Bisque was this man, and for that, I remain eternally grateful.

Afterwards, I fell asleep with Fletcher's arms around me, staring out at a pale yellow moon and thinking to myself, 'Three months, 27 days, 21 hours ...'

Word of our passionate night together got out immediately when Shermie Hempstead caught me sneaking out of Fletcher's room early the next morning. Shermie was an okay sort, and he swore to me that he would tell no one what he had seen. By lunchtime, everyone knew.

Pinky was furious. He pulled us both aside and berated us for our irresponsible and highly illegal behavior. Of course, this all had to take place in the front two thirds of the tour bus, so the redressing was not exactly private. The rest of the company pretended to study their lines while secretly hanging on every word. After Pinky finished his tirade, Fletcher calmly explained our dissatisfaction with the tour conditions while I wept in the corner. Among Fletcher's other talents, he turned out to be a marvelous orator, and by the end of his speech, the entire company had bonded with us in mutinous antipathy of Pinky, Col Weissberger, and the disastrous experience in which they had gotten themselves involved.

Pinky was a hothead, but he knew when he was outnumbered. "Fine," he conceded. "If zat's the vey you all feel, zen from here on out, I am no longer your director. Contractually, I am obligated to continue travelink mit you until ze end of ze tour, but you vill not hear a peep out of me. Run zees tour into ze ground vor all I care. My vork is over."

After that, no one much cared that I spent my every waking minute attached to Fletcher. The Farquhar sister even apologized to me, and we all became a happy, if incredibly dysfunctional, family. Pinky kept to his word, silently riding the tour out in the front seat of the bus. We would have forgotten he was there was it not for the violent attacks of flatulence that always struck him after the eggs and beans.

I grew increasingly closer to Fletcher and the whisky he provided as the tour went on. Where at first he was simply a conduit to exploring my sexuality, he became my confidante, my rock, and, let's be honest, my father figure. Fletcher was a kind, decent man who had been chewed up and spit out by the Hollywood machine. Certainly, he had self-destructive tendencies, but even in the midst of his most severe drunk, he was still nothing but tender toward me.

For the most part, I would just as soon forget the actual performances of the tour, but there were a few dates that stick in my mind. Perhaps the most vivid night in my memories was the last show of the season, the night we played the legendary Apollo Theater in Harlem. When it was founded, the Apollo played to white audiences only, but by 1935, it had become the most well-known "race" theater in the country. We were an all-white cast in blackface. From the minute we stepped into that theater, I braced myself for a chilly reception. To be sure, minstrelsy was still a popular form of theater, but this was the Apollo, the original home of black pride. Apparently, Col Weissberger, in his never-ending search for the elusive buck, had sold the show to the Apollo as featuring a cast of famous Negro stars from Hollywood. Pinky remained silent, but I could tell that he was gloating to himself over the show that was about to take place.

The curtain rose, and we launched into our rousing opening number, "De Spirit of de South." I had never before considered the political implications of the lyrics, but performing the song for the first time in front of a black audience made me feel a profound sense of embarrassment for my craft. The song went, as follows:

We works hard in de mawning
In de fields foh Massah Kurtz
N' our feets is awus throbbin'
N' our backs is awus hurt
But we don' mind 'cause we's jus'
Happy Negroes in de dirt
N' we filled up wit' dat Spirit of de South

Looking at these lyrics for the first time in decades, they still have a profound and overwhelming effect on me. Performing in front of that audience, who had come thinking they were going to see a musical revue composed for them by people like them, was one of the most painful things I have ever had to do in my career. It was then and there that I discovered my true identity-at heart, I was an abolitionist.

The song drew to a close, the music stopped, and we hit our freeze to complete silence. Upwards of 1,500 people filled the audience, and not a single one of them applauded. If the rest of the cast was panicked, they were professional enough to not show it. We went through the first few scenes as usual, tension mounting, hatred for us seething from every corner of the theater. Offstage, I could see Pinky grinning like the cat that ate the penguin.

Finally, it was time for my solo. I walked to center stage and looked out into the audience. Black face after black face met my gaze, only their black faces were real, and permanent, and when they went into a restaurant, they couldn't simply sit down and order the quail or the grouse without someone saying, "None for you, darkie!" My heart flooded with emotion as the music began. The conductor could see my hesitation, and he directed the orchestra to run through the intro again while I composed myself.

"Stop," I suddenly shouted, and the orchestra trailed off.

I walked over to stage left and grabbed a rag that was sitting just offstage. I began wiping off my makeup as I walked back to center stage. The audience rustled uncomfortably in their seats. 'What the hell is this crazy white girl doing?' they were probably thinking. At the time, I didn't know myself. All I knew was that I could not sit by and take part in this travesty any longer.

"Ladies and gentlemen, my name is Karen Jamey. My grandparents are Rosalie and Seymour Hitler, who might be better known to you as Nip n' Tuck, legendary minstrel performers."

The audience murmured in recognition. My grandparents performed in a different time, and they had a large following among older Negroes.

"I moved out to Hollywood a few months ago to become a screen actress, and, instead, I ended up getting cast in the rotten pile of garbage that we are performing for you right now."

A light chuckle wavered through the crowd. My fellow performers stared at me in horror.

"Now, I loved my grandparents very much, and I have been brought up in the minstrel tradition without ever considering how it might look from the other side. Performing in front of you tonight, my eyes are opened. I am only thirteen years old. I don't know from racism or prejudice; I just love to perform for people. But thanks to all of you, I suddenly realize that, as a performer, I have a responsibility to society. I can no longer stand here in front of you and mock your noble race."

By this time, I had completely removed the infernal cork that blackened my face and my soul. Fletcher, ever the gentleman, had picked up his own rag and was beginning to do the same.

"Now, you good people have paid a lot of money to attend a show tonight, and I fully intend to go through with the show. But as I do so, please know that I recognize that this sort of nonsense does nothing to bring our people together. Perhaps, you can open your hearts, and we can all spend the rest of the performance laughing, not at the tired jokes that compose this revue, but at the ignorance that led to their creation.

"My grandparents were minstrels, my father was a minstrel, and I was a minstrel, until tonight. Not anymore, ladies and gentlemen. The big black buck stops here."

With that, the orchestra launched into my music, and I sang the most heartfelt rendition of "Put a Lil' Plum in It" that I had ever performed. The lyrics were remarkably appropriate for the situation:

When life gives you lemons,
You should make some lemonade,
But put a lil' plum in it.
When the sun is burning down,
Take a break in the shade,
And put a lil' plum in it.
Put a lil', put a lil', put a lil' plum in it.

When the song finished, the crowd went absolutely wild, leaping to their feet in thunderous applause. Tears streamed from smiling black faces, and from my face, which was now white. The cast, who had all removed their makeup by this time, gathered around me, and we

54

embraced each other tightly. Pinky Strudels even came out from off-stage to join in the group hug, and we welcomed the sobbing Kraut warmly into our fold. Finally, Fletcher broke the circle, shouted, "On with the show!" and we continued our performance. The audience finally with us, we sang and danced our hearts out, ending the show to cheers and a very special standing ovation just for me, Karen Jamey.

After the show, the cast celebrated the end of the run with a cabal of Harlem hepsters and jazzbos at a little club around the corner from the Apollo called the Pink Lady. News of my speech had spread beyond the theater, and the Pink Lady patrons anointed me that evening as an official "sister." We all got insanely drunk on Harlem hooch, and then Fletcher and I returned to our hotel room and screwed like jackrabbits on a conjugal visit.

"Whatever will become of us, little Karen Jamey?" he asked me, as we fell asleep in each other's arms.

"Nothing, Fletcher," I told him, surprising myself with my maturity. "We both know this crazy romance can't last, not out there, not in the real world. But don't you worry, Fletcher. There will be other tours, with other underage actresses, and soon you'll forget all about me. I just have one request for you, you big, alcoholic lug. Remember me to Harlem, Fletcher. Remember me to Harlem."

I'm not sure how much of this speech Fletcher heard before he passed out, but I could swear he snored just a little bit differently that night.

Chapter Eight

Mommy and Me

The next day, the cast and crew gathered up our bags, and with the promise that our paychecks would be awaiting us in Los Angeles, we boarded a train at Pennsylvania Station for the three-day trip that would take us back home. The tour bus had mysteriously caught fire the evening before, and Col Weissberger was forced to shell out a little extra cash to send the company home on the train. I don't know anything about that fire, except that I started it.

I said my goodbyes to Fletcher over the course of those three days. Of course, Col couldn't have been bothered to buy us a sleeper car, so whenever Fletcher and I were in the mood, we took to the bathroom. It's a wonder that no one got pregnant, especially me. At that time, the pill was practically unheard of if it had even been invented, and asking a man to wear a condom was like asking a Scotsman to put on his pants.

Fletcher was understandably more broken up about the parting than I was, considering he had a lot more to lose. He had gained a nubile, attentive, young lover with a promising future career, and I had gained an alcoholic loser with nothing ahead of him but a slow descent into complete superfluousness. His entreaties became more aggressive and more desperate as the days went on.

"Please, Karen, I beg you, stay with me," he pleaded.

"Where?" I asked. "You don't even have a home."

"We'll rent something. We'll find a place. I need you, Karen. You're the only thing I have left in this world."

"Tell it to the shoeshine boy, Fletcher," I responded coldly. "Maybe if you weren't so intent on drinking yourself to sleep every night and taking advantage of children, you'd still have a career. It was fun while it lasted. If you don't stop talking about this nonsense, I'm going to have my daddy press charges as soon as we get back to Los Angeles. Now, what do you say we have one more screw for old times' sake?"

I discovered at that moment that there are few things worse than making love to a weeping man in the bathroom of a moving train. It's not that I didn't have a certain amount of affection for Fletcher, but I was realistic. I knew it couldn't last. I was a show pony, and he was a beaten-up old plow horse with a gimpy leg and an addiction to the salt lick.

Four hours later, somewhat bruised and anxious to return to normalcy, our train disembarked at the Pasadena station. I excused myself for the restroom just before the train pulled into the station and left via a door many cars away from Fletcher Bisque and the rest of the company of *The New Soul Revue*. It was the beginning stages of a pattern that would haunt me for the rest of my life. When the chips were down, I always tried the pretzels.

Daddy was waiting for me in front of the station with a smile on his face a mile wide. We had spoken most sparsely while I was away on tour. Daddy wanted to ensure that I had the full experience of being on my own, so he only allowed me to call once every month. It was this very commitment to freedom that would prove to be the undoing of our relationship. Parents, if you take away one thing from this narrative, please learn this: *children are not to be let out of your sight until they are at least 25*. Don't get me wrong, I appreciated the long leash at the time, but I can honestly say I would not have made three quarters of the mistakes in my life if I had received adequate parenting. Children don't know what to do with freedom any more than a Mexican family would know what to do with a pair of chopsticks. They go willy-nilly, chopping at everything in sight, suddenly unaware that one doesn't even need utensils to eat a taco.

Fearful that Fletcher would attack me in the parking lot, I hurried Daddy into the car, and off we drove, into the bright future of the past.

On the way home, I skimmed through the details of the tour for Daddy, leaving out my passionate affair, my near-constant drinking, and a large percentage of the truth about what actually happened. After four months of living as an irresponsible adult, I was now back to being somebody's child. It would take me awhile to adjust. Some might say I never quite did.

I noticed as I was talking that we were not heading in the direction of the Tuckered Trucker. "What gives, Pops?" I asked. It was then that I learned of our new home. A month after I left for the tour, Daddy scraped together the money to put a down payment on a small house on the outskirts of glamorous Los Feliz. I was ecstatic. No more sitting around the pool in Burbank, far from the Hollywood action. The air rushing through the window of Daddy's Buick Marquette carried with it the promise of success and just a hint of jasmine.

When we pulled into our driveway, the sweet smell of jasmine quickly turned into the deadly smell of arsenic. Standing in the driveway, waving, was a tall, fit, blond woman in an apron and enough makeup to choke a makeup-eating horse. 'That had better be the maid,' I thought to myself, although in my gut, I knew it was not.

We drove up the driveway and parked directly in front of the woman, who was still waving like a lunatic. Daddy waved back and smiled. I pursed my lips, ready for the blow that was certain to come.

"Karen," Daddy said, turning to me, "I think it's time I introduced you to your new mommy."

That knocked the wind out of me. I had expected a girlfriend. "Girlfriend," I might have been able to handle. But *mommy*? Was I to believe that my father had met a woman, fallen in love, and gotten married in the space of four months?

I was to believe exactly that, because that's exactly what happened. Her name was Shoshona, and I detested her. She was a completely untalented, aspiring actress who had been an extra on several Paramount pictures and still held onto dreams of success even though she was well beyond the age of a starlet and starting to wrinkle in all the wrong places.

We ate dinner together that evening. Shoshona tried to break through the tension that engulfed the table. Every word out of her mouth, I glared at her with a death gaze that would have killed anyone with half a brain in her head. Shoshona was lucky enough to have been spared any amount of intellectual capacity. She smiled back at me warmly and continued prattling on endlessly about whatever it was she prattled on about endlessly. I didn't listen. I was too busy plotting ways to kill her.

To make matters worse, this was the night of the Academy Awards ceremony. All I wanted to do was listen and find out if Bette was going to win for *Dangerous*. We sat around the radio as the names were announced. That year, Bette was up against such luminaries of the silver screen as Katherine Hepburn and Claudette Colbert. Daddy had quite a thing for Ms. Colbert, I imagine because she bore more than a passing resemblance to Mother. I thought her eyes were too far apart, although in retrospect, so were Bette's, and for that matter, so were Mother's. These were in the days before the effects of alcohol consumption on fetal development were understood, and faces that today might be viewed as rather Mongoloidian were then considered the height of beauty.

Shoshona had no such Mongloidian features, save for her tiny, dim-witted brain. She had beady little eyes that were too close together, and monstrous hands that clapped in ignorant bliss when Queenie Thompson's name was announced for *The Dark Angel*.

"I just loved that film," Shoshona said. "Queenie is going to win Best Actress, I'm certain of it."

"*The Dark Angel* was a piece of shit," I announced, flatly. "And Queenie Thompson can't act her way out of bed in the morning. Bette is going to win."

Shoshona was shocked, shocked at my language. "Do you let your daughter use words like that?" she asked Daddy.

"Eh, who cares," Daddy answered, unconcerned. "My money's on Claudette Colbert."

Bette won, of course, just as I knew she would. But it was a hollow victory. How could I get excited for Bette when my life was such a shambles?

I went to bed that night as low as I could get. With the tour over and no prospects for the near future, I would be stuck in the house day after day with Shoshona, lest I came up with an immediate plan for removing her or myself. I cried myself to sleep while that baboon of a woman giggled away in the next room.

The next morning I was awakened by Shoshona's shrill voice.

"Karen!" she screamed. "Your agent's here!"

I wiped the crusties from my eyes, threw on a sundress, and wandered out into the living room. Jack Scallinger stood in the doorway, grinning, hat in his hands. Upon seeing me, he held out his arms.

"C'mere, Karen-baby," he said, "and give your old Uncle Jack some sugar."

Great. Not only did I have a new mother, I had a new uncle, as well. Next thing I knew, Daddy would tell me he'd adopted the Farquhar sisters.

Jack and I sat in the living room. Shoshona lingered just out of sight in the kitchen behind us. As Jack and I talked, I used my powers of creative visualization to imagine her accidentally slipping onto a kitchen knife.

"So, Karen-baby," Jack said. "Tell me all about the tour. Was it amazing? Did you set the world on fire?"

"I set a bus on fire," I offered.

Jack broke into a phony laugh.

"You're too much, Karen-baby," he said, "too much. Now, first things first. I'm sure you've been waiting patiently to get your paycheck. And here ya' are."

He handed me an envelope, which I ripped open greedily. At $50 a week for 16 weeks, I had a great, big, fat check for $640 waiting for me, after Jack's fee. What I found in the envelope was half that amount. I stared at the paper in shock.

"Where's the rest of it, Jack?" I demanded.

"Rest of it?" Jack asked, ever the smooth-talker. I could see his game. He knew Daddy would be away at work, and he thought he could pull the old wool over my eyes because I was nothing but a little girl who didn't even graduate from high school. Jack Scallinger didn't know with whom he was messing. When it comes to money, I don't screw around.

"Yes, Jack," I answered, coldly. "I got paid $800. You receive 20% of that, or $160. You gave me a check for $320. I want the rest of my paycheck, and I want it now."

"Karen-baby," Jack said, "you're forgetting about expenses. I take 20%, plus expenses."

"What expenses?" I screamed. "What kind of expenses could you possibly have? That entire suit couldn't have cost you more than 50 cents! And where the fuck is my screen test?"

"Hey, Karen, dollface," Jack said, unfazed, "I'm working on it. These things take time. Anyway, I got good news. Col Weissberger wants you to play the leading role in his new minstrel tour, *Mammy and Pappy*. Ain't that great?"

"I DON'T DO BLACKFACE!" I exploded.

And then it hit me: Jack Scallinger was nothing but a shyster, a damned conman. I should have guessed it the minute Daddy and I walked into that rotten little office of his. That picture of Clark Gable on the wall ... who was he trying to fool? He didn't have any friends at Republic Pictures, he didn't know anyone at RKO, and he could not get me a screen test. All he could do for me was send me out on dead-end tours put on by that cheapskate Col Weissberger.

Shoshona came trotting out of the kitchen.

"Keep it down, Kare bear, kay kay?" she said. "Loud noise isn't good for mommy's skin."

"You're not my mother!" I shouted at her. "And as far as I'm concerned," I said to Jack, "you're not my agent!"

I ran out of the room, into my bedroom, and slammed the door. In the other room, I could hear Shoshona showing Jack out, bidding him good-bye in her singsong voice. I hated them both. I knew that I had to get rid of them. But how?

Suddenly, an idea popped into my head that was beyond genius, even for a girl who was preternaturally brilliant. I knew what I had to do. It would take some of my finest acting skills to pull off, but it was the only shot I had. I would kill these two birds with one stone, or more if necessary.

The next day, I took the bus out to Jack's office. He was phony as always when he saw me.

"Come in, dollface, come in," he said. "How ya' doin'?"

"Fine, Jack, fine," I said, sweetly. "Listen, I'm really sorry about my outburst yesterday. I'm just torn up about my daddy's new wife, and I'm sorry if I took it out on her. See, the thing is, she's an actress, and she told me that she would do practically anything to land an agent."

His eyebrows shot up, as did, I'm sure, his penis. Direct hit.

"Anything?" Jack asked.

"Anything," I confirmed. "When she saw you, she thought you were so handsome. And when she found out you were an agent, well, I practically had to restrain her to keep her from jumping on top of you. And that's not right, Jack. I could never let my daddy stay married to a woman like that."

Jack nodded.

"You sure couldn't, Karen," he said. "That just ain't right. A woman like that has no business being married to your upstanding father."

"That's right," I said. "Why, if she ever found out that you almost represented Queenie Thompson, there's no telling what she might do."

"It's a dirty shame," Jack murmured.

"Right. So you see, I couldn't possibly think about going on that Col Weissberger tour, not with this sort of thing going on in my life."

Jack grabbed a folder from his desk, put it over his crotch, and leaned back in his chair.

"Tell ya' what, Karen," he said. "You let me worry about your daddy's new wife. The tour doesn't start for another two weeks. By hook or by crook, we'll get you that part."

I smiled wide. "Oh, Mr. Scallinger, you're an angel," I said.

He grinned back. "Certified," he said. Sucker.

Back at home, I happened to mention to Shoshona that I had just visited with Jack, and he had asked if she was currently under representation.

"He did?" she asked, intrigued.

"He did," I answered. "See, he's casting the new Queenie Thompson film, and he was looking for an actress to play Queenie's sister. He thought you might be perfect for the part."

Shoshona's eyes widened. "He said that? That I'd be perfect?"

"Oh yes," I nodded. "It's a star-making turn, and he thinks that you're a shoe-in. But you know how these Hollywood types work. I doubt he'd even consider you unless you slept with him, and what with you being married to Daddy and all ... I told him you weren't interested."

"Oh, no, no, no," she said, shaking her head, "you didn't!"

"I did. He might still consider you, but I'm sure it would take a lot of convincing."

"Oh my gosh. Oh my gosh." Shoshona stood up and started flailing her arms like a retard with a pile of poo in her trousers. What an intelligent man like Daddy saw in this woman, I certainly could not grasp. I could only assume that he was under the mind control of some sort of sexual Mozart. But she couldn't be helped, and, much as I wished otherwise, I could empathize. No amount of love can fill that void that exists at the center of every actress, save for the love of an adoring crowd. Fame is the most powerful force in our universe, stronger than love, stronger than drugs, stronger even than God. Given the choice between fame and the promise of eternal happiness, I could name you a million people who would take the fame and hope for the best.

Under the auspices of running errands, Shoshona hustled out of the house and jumped on the bus. I would have to move quickly. I dialed up Daddy's store.

"Daddy," I wailed, "you have to help me. Jack Scallinger is planning on leaving town right now with all of the money I earned on the tour. You have to go over there and get my money back."

Nothing infuriated Daddy more than when people took advantage of him. He promised me he would take care of the problem and hung up the phone.

That night, after work, he walked in the door and threw eight 100-dollar bills at me.

"We're going to have to find you a new agent," he said.

"Okay," I answered. "Where's Mommy?"

Daddy eyed me suspiciously.

"You don't need to worry about Mommy anymore," he said.

I didn't press the issue.

Lesson learned: don't fuck with Karen Jamey.

Chapter Nine

A Difficult Adolescence

Summer soon came, and with it, the ugly spurt that I had been foolish enough to believe would never hit. The first thing that struck me was acne. By June, my face had become a veritable commune for unwanted pimples. July came, and I began to grow both taller and wider. My breasts exploded out of my chest in August, swelling into gigantic balloons that added ten pounds to my formerly delicate frame. My hair, which was filled with glorious curls as a youngster, became a tangled rat's nest cascading down an overlong neck.

I was in a state of shock. No matter what I did to make myself look pretty, it seemed I was now a lost cause. Daddy was no help.

"Boy, you're getting ugly," he said to me, one day early in the summer. "You're going to have to do something about that if you hope to become a great actress."

I burst into tears. It was cruel, but true. In just a few months, my dreams of stardom seemed all but wiped away by the merciless forces of nature. No agent would touch me in my gruesome state, and without school to occupy my time, I was doing nothing but sitting around the house, getting fat, and growing zits.

"What do I do, Daddy?" I sobbed. "What if this is it for me?"

"Calm down, pumpkin," Daddy answered. "I'm sure you'll grow out of it. But in the meantime, you need to do something with your time. If you're not gonna be learnin', ya' gotta be workin'."

Three days later, I started a part-time job as a waitress at Mr. Friendlier's Flapjack Shack, a few blocks down the road from Mr. Friendly's. In spite of my vulgar appearance, Mr. Friendlier took a shine to me, and he gave me good, solid, morning shifts where I earned a decent paycheck. I ceased to be up-and-coming screen siren Karen Jamey, and returned to being plain, old, stupid Karen Hitler.

The next two and a half years remain a rather dark period of my life that I'd just as soon forget. Although I was friendly with the other waitresses, they were all older than me, wrapped up in their own lives, which didn't include a young, fat girl with a bad complexion. When I wasn't working, I became a voracious reader, plowing through classics like *Little Women* and the other great books. From time to time, I would receive letters in the mail from Fletcher Bisque in which he would try to woo me back on the road with tales of his alcoholic adventures. I never wrote him back. I couldn't bear to think of my period in the spotlight, no matter how short-lived and unimpressive it may have been.

In 1938, with tensions heating up in Europe, the name "Hitler" suddenly found itself out of vogue in the Americas. Daddy was no dummy; he could see the way the tide was turning. On April 15 1938, just 15 days before my 16th birthday, Daddy adopted my stage name for his own, and we officially became Jebediah and Karen Jamey.

Almost immediately, my skin began to clear. By my birthday, I was five pounds lighter, and by early June, I was an attractive 5'6", 125-pound young woman, with a 34-inch bust in a C cup. One and _ months after changing my name, I had gone from ugly duckling to knockout. The only explanation, as far as I can tell, is that the cosmos were waiting all along for me to assume my true identity. If only the cosmos had thought to inform me years before, I could have saved myself and many others a lot of suffering. They could have found a much nicer way to alert me than the Holocaust.

"You're not ugly anymore," Daddy remarked one day, ever observant. "Might be time for you to try to get an agent again."

But how? I was so far out of the game I could barely even recognize the ball.

As happened so often in my life, the sticky tendrils of fate tapped me on my shoulder when I least expected them. Early one July morning at Mr. Friendlier's, a familiar looking man with a shuffling strut entered the restaurant, flanked by two large gentlemen in sunglasses. They were all sharply dressed in expensive-looking Italian suits, an unusual sight in the Flapjack Shack at 7 a.m. I walked over to their table. As I was handing them their menus, the familiar-looking man stared at me intensely.

"I know you," he said.

"You know me," I answered.

"Tony Tarantella," he said.

That's where I'd seen him before.

"Oh!" I replied, without thinking. "The gangster!"

At that, Tony's men broke into peals of tommy gun laughter. Tony held up his hand and the laughter ceased immediately.

"I am an independent business man," he said slowly, "and you are a beautiful young woman. What do you do ..." glancing at my nametag then back up into my face, "Karen?"

"I'm a waitress," I replied.

"So you are," Tony agreed, fixating his blue-gray eyes directly on mine. "What do you *really* do?"

His gaze bore through me like a sword made of razor-sharp butter, and I felt something I had not felt in many years-*desire*. Tony Tarantella was a handsome man, somewhere in his mid-40s, I was guessing, by his salt and pepper hair. He had the rough skin and suppressed smile of a man who has seen a lot in his lifetime. He was stocky, but not fat; deliberate, but not slow. I wanted to climb on top of him and ride his cock until it exploded.

"I'm ... I'm an actress," I stammered.

"Yes, you are," Tony said, nodding. "And there is no reason for you to be working here in this place. Ya' wanna make some real money?"

He handed me a business card. "The Exclusive: A Gentleman's Club," it read, with an address and phone number. On the backside of the card was an embossed line drawing of a girl with long, flowing hair and high-heeled boots sitting in a martini glass. Under the picture, the card read, "Tony Tarantella: Proprietor."

"Every agent, every casting director, every star in Hollywood comes to my club," Tony said. "Some of the most famous actresses in the world started their careers working for me. You got something special, Karen. I'm gonna be at the club tomorrow from ten until one, and I expect to see you there. Now, please bring me the steak and eggs."

His two toadies nodded.

"Steak and eggs," they said in unison.

The next day I drove out to the Exclusive in the beat-up used Buick I bought with my waitressing money. The Exclusive was housed in a nondescript building on Sunset, about a mile away from Mr. Friendlier's. The only indicator that I was in the right place was a small sign next to the front door bearing the martini-girl logo from the business card.

I parked the car and knocked on the door. No response. I knocked again. A few moments later, a slot opened at the top of the door. Behind the slot, a shifty pair of eyes peeked out into the L.A. sun.

"Wachyawant?" came a gruff voice from behind the door. I could only assume that the voice belonged to the same person who owned the eyes.

"I'm here to see Mr. Tarantella," I said.

The shifty eyes stopped shifting and slowly took me in from head to toe, or, rather, from upper breast to chin, which was about as far as their range of vision probably extended.

"Wachyername?" came the gruff voice again.

"Karen Jamey," I said. "From Mr. Friendlier's."

The slot banged shut. I waited nervously outside the door, not quite knowing into what I was getting. My years as a troll had punctured enormous holes in the unwavering self-confidence I had as a youngster, and now I felt as though I was a bruised cherub, anxiously waiting for St. Peter to let me into his magnificent kingdom. At the same time, I recognized that I was playing with fire. Tony Tarantella was hardly the sort of person one wanted to get mixed up with were one hoping to live the Christian life. I had no such ideals, having endured an unfortunate accident at a church bake sale some years prior with my hobo mother's candied yams, which set-off a chain reaction of events that ended with Mother denouncing the church and most likely dooming our family to an afterlife of eternal suffering. Sad, is it not, what havoc can be wrought by a plate of candied yams?

After waiting a few more moments, the door swung open, and I was welcomed inside by Tony Tarantella.

"Good to see you, Karen," he said. "You're a smart girl who has made a wise choice."

"Thank you, Mr. Tarantella," I said, "but I haven't chosen anything yet."

Tony smiled. I could tell he went in for the tough-girl act. If I was really an actress, now was the time to prove it.

The "club," as it were, looked little different from any number of Italian restaurants in L.A., save for the total absence of windows. Tony led me to a little round table next to the stage at the far end of the front room. Across the room, near the bar, three or four swarthy-looking characters shot craps while a handful of beautiful women looked on, quietly. Those men weren't the only ones rolling the dice that day. I was, too. With my future. In case you didn't understand the analogy.

"Sit down," Tony said, and I sat. When Tony Tarantella told you to do something, you did it. He had that commanding, Buck Rogers presence about him, that steely-eyed look that made you want to ...

Goddammit! This fucking cat ... Myrna, if you don't tell your goddamned stinky cat to stop jumping on me when I'm talking ... I'm dictating the story of my life, Myrna, that's what! Yeah, well, it's a lot more interesting than your stupid life! What, did you work in a fucking factory for 40 years? And then you retired and got your fucking pension? Fascinating, Myrna. I'm sure they're going to be writing all about your life, next. I'm an actress, you stupid cow. You can go choke on your idiot cat for all I care.

I'm sorry, where was I? Oh yes, Tony Tarantella, and the Buck Rogers presence. Ugh, whatever you want to write is fine with me. The train of thought is lost. Suffice it to say that Tony Tarantella was a man, in the way that we women claim we don't like but are undeniably attracted to all the same. Being ignored by Tony Tarantella was more exciting than being ravished by the most attentive, sensitive lover, and being ravished by Tony Tarantella was, well, we'll save that story for a later time.

"How old are you?" Tony asked.

"Nineteen," I lied.

Tony cracked a smile.

"Bullshit you're nineteen. You're sixteen. Ya' know how I know? *I know.*"

I nodded.

"Yes," I said, seeing no reason to continue the charade. "I'm six-teen."

Tony leaned back in his chair and lit up a gigantic cigar. He chewed on the end and stared at me thoughtfully. I could feel the rush of desire overtaking me again, only this time I didn't turn away. I stared him straight in the eyes with a poker face that was barely tough enough for solitaire. He chuckled under his breath.

"You're a tough little cookie, ain't ya'?" he asked. "Ya' seen a lot, little girl, and I can respect that. But what do I do with you? Anyone finds out I got a 16 year-old kid working in my club, I'll be shut down faster'n you can say 'Jack Robinson.'"

"It's not work if it's done for pleasure," I said, seductively.

Tony continued to stare at me with an unreadable expression on his face, absorbing the situation like a sponge. I could bet that there was a brilliant mind not far behind those blue-gray eyes.

"Who's gonna bother you about it, anyway?" I offered. "You're Tony Tarantella."

"All right," he finally said, "ya' got the job. Ya' do three dances a night, three nights a week. The rest of the time, ya' mingle and make the men feel good about themselves. Club opens at nine; you should be here at eight. We close at two, with occasional after-hours parties on the weekend. Come in for training this Saturday and Sunday during the day; I'll have some of the girls show ya' the ropes. It ain't rocket science. Smart girl like you oughta pick it up immediately. I'm gonna have ya' start out Monday through Wednesday, and if ya' do a good job, I'll give ya' some weekends. Only rules here are one, show up on time, and two, no sleeping with the clientele. Ya' think you can handle that?"

"That depends," I said. "Are you the clientele?"

Tony barked out a hoarse laugh.

"You're gonna go far, Karen Jamey," he said.

"Freddie!" he shouted across the room. "Bring us some menus!"

"Now," he continued, to me, "I understand ya' gotta be tough when you come in for an interview like this, but ya' got the job, and now I wanna see the real you. Freddie's gonna make us some lunch, and I don't bullshit during lunch. You understand?"

I nodded. He sat forward in his chair, leaning in close to my face.

"I know you ain't as tough as ya' look, Karen," he whispered. "You got pain inside ya'. I can see it in your eyes. Now, let's cut the shit and get to know each other. Howsat sound?"

My heart fluttered. I had a feeling Tony Tarantella didn't open up to just anyone. He was completely wrong, of course. I had no pain inside me. What did I care? Save for a few years of looking like a Halloween costume, a horrible tour experience, the death of my grandparents, the loss of my mother, the complete absence of friends, and my burgeoning propensity for alcoholism, I had led a charmed life. Still, it was sweet for Tony to try, and if he wanted pain, I could give him pain. It was part of my training.

Freddie came over with a couple of menus and a bottle of wine. As he poured us each a glass, I scanned the menu for the item I knew I had to order.

"Anything ya' want, Karen," he said. "I recommend the pasta fagioli."

"Then that's what I shall have," I said, closing my menu. "But first, I'd like to start with the chowder."

Tony blinked.

"No chowder, darling," he said. "Try the minestrone."

Chapter Ten

Dancing Queen

I knew Daddy wouldn't approve of me working in a dancehall, so I told him I had been hired for the night shift at a restaurant in Pasadena.

"Why the devil would you want to work all the way over there?" he asked.

"It's only a few miles farther, Daddy," I said. "And it's a much nicer restaurant. The tips are a lot better."

"Fine," Daddy said. "But you need to start thinking about your acting career, Karen. You're too beautiful and talented to waste your best years working in restaurants."

"I know, Daddy," I agreed. "Trust me; this is a good career move. A lot of famous people come into this restaurant. I'll be signed to a three picture deal before you know it."

Daddy snorted. He was used to the old ways of doing business, where getting to the top involved hard work and climbing the ladder. He didn't understand that in Hollywood, careers could be made and broken over a plate of key lime pie, or any type of pie, really. The proof was all over the pages of *Photoplay*. If Lana Turner could be discovered in a drugstore, and Hedy Lamarr could be discovered in a women's prison, then I could be discovered waiting tables. Only, I wouldn't be waiting tables, I would be dancing atop them.

With my father appeased thusly, I returned to The Exclusive that

Saturday for a crash course in seductive dancing. My tutors were both very nice and intensely stupid. They did know their business, though, and they taught me a number of tricks for milking the tips out of the customers. The dancing itself was not difficult ... in those days, we didn't have any elaborate pole or trapeze setups to contend with. The height of complexity in the burlesque era was the ability to swing one's tassels, which, really, any idiot with strong back muscles and a pair of tits could quickly master. Dancing in those days relied much more on acting skills than sexual proclivity. The key, as my tutors explained, was to seduce every gentleman in the joint with your eyes. Too much eye contact made men embarrassed; not enough left them disinterested. "Think of it as the sort of flirtation that might take place on a bus or a train," advised Sheena, one of my teachers. "That shy, occasional contact you make with a gentleman's eyes ... you pretend to be reading your newspaper, but ever so often you glance back to see that he's still looking, and of course, he is, because he thinks that if he stares closely enough, you may rise from your seat and attack him with fiery passion. That's who you must be to every man in this joint-the flirtatious girl on the train. Only half-naked."

The cultivation of a persona was a necessity-every man's fantasies differed, and The Exclusive aimed to appeal to a broad range of customers. Sheena, for instance, was the Jungle Woman; her costumes included a lot of leopard and tiger prints. Janine was the Bad Girl; she wore leather and carried a chain that she would beat against the stage for effect. Tanya was the Exotic Princess; she dressed like an Indian woman and did a lot of belly dancing. My persona was to be the Naughty School Girl, a role that I was only too eager to assume, considering I had missed out on my formative school years. It was also a brilliant disguise; no one would ever suspect that the woman who went out of her way to look like jailbait was actually jailbait.

Persona established, we spent the next two days coming up with fitting routines. It was all quite innocent stuff by today's standards ... a lot of thumb sucking and coy looks. The only part that gave me a slight pause was the removal of my shirt at the end of each routine. But even that was rather innocent; as was the law at the time, most of my breasts had to be covered, so all the men were really getting that they couldn't see from a trip to the beach was a small portion of the tops and bottoms of my breasts and my bare midriff. Granted, at the time, I certainly wouldn't be welcomed in church in that sort of uniform, but I was so pleased to finally have something to show off that I really didn't give a good goddamned that I was being risqué. The notion of men ogling my body made me quite tingly, in fact … which is probably as good an indicator as any that I was too young and naïve for this world I was entering. From what I had seen of the world, the worst a man could do was fall in love with me. Well, believe you me, I now recognize that men are capable of far more dangerous things than love, if they are even capable of that.

I arrived at eight the next Monday night to prepare for my big debut. I will admit, although I was confident that I knew my routine, I was quite nervous, it having been some time since I last graced the stage. The other girls were extremely supportive, though, and thank God for it, because I was shaking like an epileptic Chihuahua.

"You'll be fine, honey," Sheena consoled me, as she slipped into a leopard-print bustier. "The men are going to eat you up."

"Oh!" Lydia, the Ditzy Blonde exclaimed. "Is Fatty Arbuckle in the audience tonight?"

The other girls laughed.

"I hope not," I joked. "I'm in no mood to get raped to death!"

The other girls did not laugh quite so hard at that one.

My first dance was to be performed at 10:30. Whenever a new girl arrived, the girls informed me, Tony liked to make a big production out of it. Many of the men who attended The Exclusive were regulars, and a new girl to them was like a new pacifier to a baby. I was not allowed on the floor until after my dance, because Tony didn't even want them to get a glimpse of me until I took the stage. At 9:00, I stood backstage and peeked out of the curtain at Lydia's routine to get a feel for the crowd. From what I could tell, they were totally without emotion. Lydia danced her heart out to a smattering of applause. Although it was difficult to see beyond the stage lights, there looked to be no more than ten people in the crowd.

While I stood and watched the stage, Tony snuck up behind me and grabbed me around the waist. I let out a small shriek of surprise.

"Come, come, little Karen," he whispered in my ear. "Back to the dressing room with you."

He led me back to the dressing room, where five or six girls were lounging in various states of undress.

"Hello, ladies," Tony said. "I trust you are all taking care of my precious little angel here?"

"Oh, yeah, Tony," Sheena said, sarcastically. "We've got her wings straightened out and her halo polished."

"Good," Tony smiled. "You look like a million bucks, Karen," he said to me. "You're really gonna knock 'em dead tonight."

"From the looks of things, they're dead already," I quipped.

"It's early on a Monday," Tony said. "Come 10:30, this joint'll be jumpin', I promise you. Some of the boys are real anxious to see you dance, yours truly included."

"Yeah, well, I'm anxious for it to be over," I said.

Tony gave me a peck on the cheek and left me to my nerves.

"Oh-la-la," Sheena said, sidling up next to me. "Looks like someone's sweet on you. Who woulda thunk it? Tony Tarantella, all-American boy-next-door."

"Yeah, boy-next-door, all right," I answered. "Next door to the prison."

An hour later I stood backstage, bouncing up and down with fear and excitement. The audience had filled out, and I felt a sense of anticipation drifting from the crowd. At 10:30 on the dot, Tony Tarantella walked out on stage with a microphone.

"Hey, Tony," shouted a voice from the crowd, "ya' ain't gonna dance for us, are ya'?"

"Nah," Tony snapped, "the only place I'm dancin' is on your grave."

The crowd exploded with laughter. Although we were the entertainment, Tony was clearly the star of the Exclusive.

"All right, ya' mugs," Tony said. "are ya' ready for the highlight of the evening?"

The crowd hooted and whistled.

"Then let me proudly introduce you to The Exclusive's newest find: Karen, the Naughty Schoolgirl!"

On cue, I flung the curtains apart as the band launched into a swinging version of Benny Goodman's "Goody-Goody." I bounced out to center-stage in time with the music and launched into a Lindy hop, smiling bashfully. The crowd spooned it up like a bowl of iced cream. I began my scan of the room, as the other girls had instructed. I nearly froze in place when I saw who was sitting at the front table, just to the left of the stage-none other than Clark Gable, Robert Taylor, and Spencer Tracy. I gave each one of them the doe-eyes, then turned my back and slowly began unbuttoning my blouse. Still with my back turned, my blouse fully unbuttoned, I bent over quickly, so that my schoolgirl skirt flipped up, my panties exposed to the audience. I peeked through my legs and flashed a surprised look at the table of megastars. Clark, the old wolf, stood up and let out a high-pitched whistle, and I felt a surge of confidence the likes of which I've seldom known. Giving myself over to the music, I twisted around and dropped to my knees. I took my shirt off, twirled it over my head, and threw it into the crowd, who descended upon it like a pack of rabid jackals. I still had an undershirt on, which snapped up the back. Rising from the stage, I arched my back, and the snaps started to give way. I shook my head around, pigtails flapping, breasts jiggling, and then suddenly, in one quick move, I slid the undershirt off my body and threw it to the side of the stage. The crowd screamed with desire. All three stars were on their feet now, stomping and clapping along with the music. In the back, I caught Tony's eyes, and I did not let them go. Standing on the stage in nothing but a skirt and a satin bra, I motioned to Tony to join me. He walked up on the stage, in the thrall of my sexual power. As soon as he climbed onto the stage, I whispered in his ear, "Protect me." As the song ran through the final chorus, I turned to face Tony, my back to the crowd, reached between my breasts and unsnapped my brassiere. Tony got the picture, in more ways than one. He reached behind me, ripped off the bra, then grabbed my hands and spun me around, taking care to cover my breasts with his arms just as I turned completely to the front. The band hit the final note and the whole place leapt to its feet, filling the air with wild applause. Tony and I each let out a giant, relieved laugh, and I snuggled back into his warm arms as he dragged me off stage.

Backstage, Tony spun me around and planted a passionate kiss upon my lips. Something stiff pressed against my leg. At first I thought it was an erection, and I got a little bit wet. Then I decided it was a gun, and I got a little bit wetter.

He pushed me away lightly and let me put my brassiere back on. I was still giggling from the thrill of the moment. He was smiling wide. Behind us, the crowd screamed, "More! More!"

"You're trouble, Karen Jamey," he said to me, chuckling.

"So are you," I answered, flashing the bedroom eyes.

He ignored my attempts at seduction. "Usually, after the girls get done dancing, you're supposed to go out there and work the crowd. I don't think that's wise for you right now. I'll pay ya' double, but you're done dancin' for tonight. Never give 'em too much of a good thing. Now, go get dressed."

"But," I protested, "what about ..."

"The gentlemen in the front row?" he asked. "Yeah, I know, ya' wanna do some star-gazing. Forget it. They're in here all the time. You'll meet 'em soon. You're gonna be a star, Karen."

I blushed. Tony slipped past me and walked onto the stage.

"Calm down, ya' bastards," he said. "Karen's here every Friday and Saturday night. Ya' want more? Come back this weekend."

In one night, I had gone from neophyte to weekend star of The Exclusive, the most famous dance club in all of Hollywood. I was back, baby, and this time, I wasn't going down without a fight.

Chapter Eleven

So Long, Daddy Dear

I drove home that night, my pockets full of cash, and my heart full of wanton lust. When I walked in the door, Daddy was waiting for me on the davenport, a glass of bourbon in his hand. This was unusual, because Daddy rarely drank, and when he did, he never drank alone.

"Daddy?" I asked. "Are you all right?"

He stared straight ahead, as if comatose. Slowly, he lifted his head to look me in the face with eyes that were red from crying. My blood ran cold, terrified that Daddy had discovered my secret.

"Daddy?" I whispered. "What is it?"

Suddenly, his face broke into a smile, amid the tears.

"The hospital called," Daddy finally said. "Your grandfather is going to be okay."

"Oh, Daddy!" I shouted, leaping into his arms. I broke into joyous tears, and we held each other tightly, crying, for a long, long time.

The next morning, Daddy left for Baltimore. Although I was terribly anxious to see Grandpapa, I was even more anxious at the prospect of having the home to myself. I kissed Daddy good-bye on the stairs, with the promise that I would be out to Baltimore as soon as I could get some time off work. Minutes after he left, I was in my car and on my way to the Exclusive.

The eyes at the door gave me no hassle this time. The door

opened, and I strode inside confidently. I walked straight back to Tony's table, where he was sipping espresso with three other large gentlemen.

"Hello, Karen," he said, coolly. The other three men scanned me with wolf eyes.

"Can I speak to you in private, Tony?" I asked. Tony nodded. The other men scattered.

I pulled a chair up to Tony, as close as I could get.

"My Daddy just went out of town," I cooed, placing my hand on his thigh. "And I'm feeling lonely."

Tony drained his espresso and slammed the cup down on the table.

"Let's go," he said.

We went back to the house. I fumbled with the key in the lock as Tony stood behind me, kissing my neck. I finally got the door open and we piled into the living room, straight back to the davenport, where Tony laid me down. I unbuttoned his fly while he slipped my dress off my shoulders. Slipping my hand into his drawers, I grabbed his penis, and was startled to discover that, contrary to my expectations, Tony Tarantella was not packing. To put it bluntly, he was hung like a peanut.

At the time, I didn't realize just how small he was. I had only seen one other penis in my time, and I was pretty certain that one was a monster. I didn't know what an average penis looked like. But my God, Tony Tarantella was small.

No matter. By now he had me stripped bare, and I was willing to work with whatever tool he had to offer. Although we had no name for it at the time, Tony introduced me to the concept of foreplay. Fletcher was always content to tie one on and ram it home, which was all well and good for him, but left me a little high and dry most of the time. Tony Tarantella, on the other hand, now there was a lover. He was gentle, soothing, patient. What he lacked in package he more than made up for in tenderness.

I stretched out across the davenport and pulled his warm body into me. Cradling me in his arms, he gently thrust himself inside my warm and tender loins. His penis was like a divining rod pointing straight into the source of my pleasure. Deep within, my inner brook boiled and swirled, growing steadily hotter, hungrier, more bellicose. He played his tiny penis around the lips of my vagina, sending me into an erotic frenzy. "Now!" I shouted. "I must have you, my darling! Give it to me, you insane, guinea bastard!" Then he stuck it in and fucked me really fast. It was one of the happiest moments of my life, and, to this day, one of my fondest memories. I felt as though Tony and I were cut from the same cloth, a swath of velvet, perhaps, or maybe some sort of lovely Japanese silk.

At the end of our love making, I showed Tony to the door. He left me with a lingering kiss and the promise that he would return that night, after finishing with his business affairs.

I was absolutely on cloud nine. Poor, naïve, stupid me. I truly believed that Tony and I were in the beginning stages of a love affair that would last for an eternity. I have always been a romantic, at heart. Even today, when Myrna is droning on about her stupid dead husband and her lousy children who never visit her, I say to her, "That's fine, dear, I'm sure that to you, your 45-year marriage to boring old Frank was satisfactory, but I have known passion so intense, so incredible, it would kill someone like you."

I was on cloud ten after our next session that very evening. Everything Tony did to me once in the morning, he did twice at night. He awoke in me passions unlike any I'd ever known, as though he had an invisible passion ray that shot directly into my vagina.

"I could lie here like this forever," I said, as we lay on the bed, smoking post-coital cigarettes.

"Me too," he said. "But I can't. I gotta get home to the wife. I'll see ya' on Friday, Toots."

The news that Tony was married came as somewhat of a shock to me. I felt as though I had awakened for my morning shower, only to find a family of greased monkeys prancing about in the tub. Tony didn't wear a ring, and I had never heard him mention a wife before. Granted, I had only known him for a week. But one usually gets these things out in the open before one has intercourse. Or, rather, one rarely does.

I said nothing to him as he left. I was at a loss for anything to say. It was through this experience that I learned one of the most valuable lessons of my life: few things are ever as they seem, and if a man seems too good to be true, you're probably psychotic.

The next Friday, I showed up at the club with every intention of putting an end to the Tony Tarantella affair before it really began.

I noticed when I stepped into the dressing room that something was a bit off. The chatter of the other dancers ceased as soon as I walked in the room. I walked over to my station. The other dancers, who just last week were gathered about me in encouragement, would not even look me in the eye. Never one to mince words, I thought it best to get everything out on the table.

"All right, yes, it's true," I said. "Tony and I are having an affair. I know what you're all thinking. You're thinking that I seduced him and I'm taking advantage of his position to get ahead in the club and take your prime spots. Well, nothing could be further from the truth. It's been years since I felt a sense of community. Since starting here, I have come to know and love each and every one of you, and I beg of you, I plead that you give me a second chance. I can't help it that I'm young and beautiful and talented and the owner of the club loves me. What I can do, however, is put an end to my relationship with Tony, in the spirit of solidarity. It's all over tonight, girls. I'm going to talk to Tony and tell him that I don't want to continue this nonsense any longer. Yes, I will admit to you, I do have a bit of a soft spot for the big lug, but nothing is as important to me as the friendship and support of you all, my comrades-in-tassles, as it were.

"As for getting the coveted Friday and Saturday night slots; that, I'm afraid, I cannot control. I am gifted. I shall continue to dance to the full extent of my abilities. Would you ask Beethoven to write an average symphony? Would you ask Shakespeare to write a comedy? You might, but you shouldn't, ladies. That's the point. You shouldn't."

When I was finished speaking, I stood, leaning on the makeup counter, waiting for the rush of applause that did not come. My words hung heavy in the room. Each woman had stopped her pre-show ritual to listen and consider what I had said. They looked to each other, helpless. Could it be that this neophyte, this self-assured teenager, had broken through their catty outer shells and touched their hearts?

Sheena the Jungle Woman was the first one to speak up.

"Tony dumped me for you," she said dryly.

"Me too," seconded Rose the French Maid.

"Me three," thirded Janine the Bad Girl.

"He dumped me," said Tanya the Exotic Princess. "Said what he had with you was too special."

"He said the same thing to me," chimed in Ethel the Fat One.

"You, Ethel?" asked Rose. "I didn't even know you and he ..."

"You don't remember?" replied Ethel. "You joined us once! In the boathouse!"

"Oh, that was you?" asked Rose, surprised. "Did you change your hair?"

"I've been going to a new girl," Ethel admitted. "She's a little more expensive, but she really has a nice eye."

"Wait ... everyone ... stop," I said, befuddled. "You're telling me that Tony was cheating on his wife with *all* of you? And that now he's broken up with *all* of you so that he can date me exclusively?"

"Well, he didn't break up with me," chirped Lydia the Ditzy Blonde from the corner. "But I missed the staff meeting on Wednesday."

Just then, Tony poked his head in the dressing room.

"Lydia, can I talk to you for a minute?" he asked. Then, spying me, with a warm smile, "Oh, hello, Karen."

"Hello, Tony," I nodded, stone faced.

Lydia left the room to have her conversation, and I looked around the room at the other girls, helplessly. We all stood, awkward and silent, waiting for someone to speak up. At that moment, knowing I was at the end of my rope, I fell back on the one thing I had left to offer-youth and inexperience. I broke into a rainstorm of tears.

"I'm just a little girl!" I wailed.

The other dancers instantly dropped their attitudes and crowded around me, clasping me in their arms. Together, we had a good, cleansing cry, until one-by-one, they pulled away and resumed their costuming rituals.

"I ain't never seen anything like it, Karen," whistled Rose, when the dressing room had returned to normal. "Tony ain't never acted like this before. He's like a little puppy dog when someone mentions your name. I don't know what you done to him, but he sure liked it."

"What do I do, Rose?" I asked.

"I don't know, kiddo. Do you love him?"

"With all my heart and soul," I answered, not really believing a word of it.

"Then go to him, Karen," she said. "Go to him and confess your feelings."

While I was performing my dances that evening, I glanced up from time to time to see Tony standing near the bar, staring at me with an unreadable expression on his face. As before, the crowd reaction was palpable. Men hooted and whistled, standing on their chairs, screaming my name every time I was onstage. When I was not on stage, the other girls reported tepid audience reactions. If I had doubts before about my attractiveness, they were finally erased that evening.

After my last dance, Tony pulled me aside and planted a passionate kiss upon my lips.

"Listen, Tony," I said. "We need to talk."

"You're damn right," Tony said. "I want you to stop dancing."

His words hit me like a ton of bricks wrapped in a ton of feathers.

"But ... I just started," I said.

"I don't care. You're fired. I can't have my best girl dancing on stage in front of a bunch of jackals."

"But ..." I protested, "you let your other best girls dance on stage in front of a bunch of jackals."

"That's different, Karen," he said. "Those girls, they were but a trifle. I love you, don't you see? I love you, Karen Jamey."

"What about your wife?" I pursed.

"What about her? She don't care. Long as I give her enough of an allowance to keep her in furs and nylon stockings, she's happy."

"Why don't you get a divorce?"

"What, are you crazy?" he asked. "I'm Catholic!"

Chapter Twelve

Life with Tony

My dancing career behind me, I now settled into the role of being Tony Tarantella's fulltime mistress. I didn't mind. The work was pretty easy, and it paid better than anything I'd done previously.

Daddy checked in every other night from Baltimore. Grandpapa was progressing in his recovery. A person's body, I learned, deteriorates considerably when not in use. All of those unused muscles and joints have to be reawakened and invited back into the world, one small step at a time. It would take a few months, Daddy told me, before Grandpapa would return to the walking and talking version we loved so.

My days were filled with leisure and leisure activities, like dancing around a room or watching Tony play golf. Nights were spent at exotic nightclubs and glamorous parties. Tony introduced me to the crème de la crème of the Hollywood crime world. Tony knew everyone who was anyone, and everybody owed Tony a favor.

Unfortunately, I was still not quite where I wanted to be. The studios at this time did everything they could to protect their stars, and being seen in the presence of a known gangster like Tony Tarantella was against strict company policy. Tony ran with the people behind the scenes; the people who made the happenings happen. People like Lucky Tufay, who was a silent founding partner in one of the first major film studios, the Jesse L. Lasky Feature Play Company; or, as it was now known, Paramount. People like Cordelia D'arger, the notorious Russian Countess and art financier. They all seemed dreadfully old and dull to me, although, to be fair, Countess D'arger did make a smashing margarita.

Things with Tony weren't all wine and roses, either. The thrill of sleeping with a criminal wears off rather quickly, especially when you're young and eager to experience the sins of the flesh and the gentleman in question is an old bag. Perhaps if Tony had been a brilliant wit, I might have forgiven his lack of passion, but I quickly found our conversations lacking in substance. Tony was a smart man if you needed directions or somebody killed, but he was a zero when it came to popular culture. His snide remarks in the presence of my gossip magazines drove me up the wall.

"Why don't you read something what stimulates your head?" he asked me once.

"What do you read?" I shot back. "Gangster magazines?"

"I read the classics," he sniffed.

The classics, according to Tony, were Beatrix Potter's series of books for children and *Bambino,* the best-selling biography of George Herman "Babe" Ruth. According to his bookshelf, anyway. He claimed that he'd read Jane Austen, but I didn't believe she was a real author. I have since learned otherwise, of course. She is a real person and she's written some fine books, not the least of which is one of my all time favorites, *Little Women.*

But, oh! There were some good times, as well. I remember vividly a costume ball thrown by the Countess at her luxurious home in Hollywoodland. I went as Titania, the Greek goddess of whispers. Tony was my Aeschylon, the multi-headed, frog-legged creature who was Titania's abusive lover.

The Countess, being a scholar in the ancient myths, recognized us at once. She ushered us into her expansive front front room. The normal names for rooms cease to apply when you are among the ultra-wealthy. You may have an inordinate number of bathrooms, bedrooms, closets, and the like, but what becomes of the poor living room? The family room? The den? Tossed aside, in favor of such unfriendly names as "front front room" and "left side back room, right."

We made our way into the downstairs front kitchen, where the bar had been set up for the evening. I had felt the pull as I walked in the door, and I knew this was the place. And there she was, standing next to the bar, sipping a pina colada, esteemed siren of the silver screen, Ms. Bette Davis.

Since our first meeting, lo those many years before, I had grown quite a bit, in both stature and confidence. While I still felt the magnetic pull of celebrity, I suddenly realized that I no longer noticed it as much as I had in my younger days. I understood with this realization why Bette's gravitational pull no longer had such an effect on my body. It was because I had developed my own magnetic force field. Soon, others would be feeling my presence.

It was a liberating realization, and to celebrate, I walked straight up to Ms. Davis and said, "Hello."

"Do I know you, dear?" she asked me.

"I believe so," I answered. "I'm Karen Jamey. We met at Musso & Frank."

"Ugh," she replied. "Dreadful place. I haven't been there in years."

"Actually," I said, "the chowder's quite good."

She nodded.

"They do have a nice chowder."

And like that, we were the best of friends. For the next ten minutes, we shared a warm, insightful conversation about the evolution of acting, just two old stagehands talking shop. And then she passed out in the sink. It was a remarkable moment, and one that I shall cherish forever.

The rest of the night was spent dancing and laughing with Tony's exotic friends. The Commander of the Armed Forces of Guatemala told us the most delightful story about a little friend of his named Mulgar, who delivered mail at the government building. Mulgar's growth had been stunted due to an unfortunate run-in with the polio virus as a boy, so as a fully grown adult, he only stood three and a half feet tall. But he was scrappy, and friendly, and the Commander took a shine to him.

For Mulgar's 18th birthday, the Commander and his friends at the base decided to pull a little prank. While he was on his daily paper route, the Commander asked Mulgar to stop by. In his office, the Commander had assembled the head of police and the owner of the newspaper that Mulgar delivered. When Mulgar came in, the Commander gravely informed him that he had been fingered as a spy by Guatemalan intelligence. "Non, non," Mulgar protested. "Non, non, non!" The Commander told him it was too late, he was to be placed before a firing squad immediately.

Now, anyone with any sense knows that governments don't just go about placing people in front of firing squads without just cause, but Mulgar, as the Commander explained, was a little bit slow. So, when they blindfolded him and stood him against the wall, he was shaking with fear. It was all the Commander could do, he said, to keep a straight face.

The Commander gave the signal, and Mulgar dropped to the ground, terrified. As soon as he dropped, the firing squad shot their pistols into the air and launched into a rousing chorus of the Guatemalan birthday song. Well, as the Commander put it, little Mulgar was simply tickled pink by all the attention, and he joined the men for cake and ice cream after being fitted with a fresh pair of pants.

The notion of this little Guatemalan man crapping his pants sent me into hysterics, so much so that Tony had to call in the paramedics to make sure I was okay. Which I was, of course, no thanks to those idiots with their probing medical devices.

It was around about January of 1939 when I started to feel that my problems with Tony were irreconcilable. I was in a bit of a sore spot, what with him being a notoriously hot-tempered gangster and all. It was at this point that a face from the past came back in my life with devastating consequences.

The night, I recall, was a stormy one, filled with the same sense of foreboding and dread that a storm always seems to bring in the pictures. I was snuggled in my pajamas in the sitting room, listening to an episode of my favorite radio drama, *The Rites of Passion,* when a knock came on the door. I was unaccustomed to visitors, so the knock came as a bit of a surprise. I knew that Tony would be at the Exclusive until at least midnight, it being the Thursday before Yom Kippur, and Jews being horny. I answered the door nonetheless, eager to see who would be knocking on my door when I did not expect a knocking.

On the other side of the door, wet hat in shivering hand, a man stood with his head lowered in shadows. As the door swung gently open, a flourish of strings flew from the hinges and pierced the stormy night air. The man lifted his face slowly, slowly, until his eyes connected with mine. High in the air above us, the strings swelled into a gorgeous chord, swirling the sounds of the rain and thunder into itself like a musical tornado, and bringing with it a lightning bolt that illuminated the sky behind the body of the man standing on my front porch-Fletcher Bisque.

I gasped and swooned slightly at the drama of it all. Fletcher reached a wet hand across the invisible barrier of the doorframe, bringing it to rest upon my cheek. I shivered in turn from the coldness of his touch and the desire that burbled within me. Fletcher looked good, with a renewed clarity and strength that were not present in the man I remembered.

"My darling, my darling," Fletcher cooed, staring deep into my eyes.

"You poor thing," I said. "You must be absolutely freezing."

"Nothing a trip inside your loins won't cure," Fletcher replied.

I blushed.

"Come in, Fletcher. Let's get you dried off."

I gave Fletcher some dry clothes from Daddy's closet. While he changed, I lit a fire and poured us some bourbon, and soon after, we were sitting on the sofa, catching up on our years apart. A few months prior, it seemed, out on tour with yet another pile of musical trash, Fletcher had endured a psychological breakdown. The pressures of a life spent in meaningless pursuit of fame and drink had taken their toll on his psyche. For days, he remained locked in a hotel room in Albany, refusing to act or speak with anyone. To clear his mind, he began writing a screenplay, loosely based on our relationship.

The tour moved on without him, but Fletcher stayed, pouring his emotions into the script. The screenplay had fallen into the hands of a powerful agent, who went absolutely bonkers for the tender love story of a man and an underage girl. Fletcher promptly quit the tour and returned to Los Angeles, one day before showing up on my doorstep. The next morning, he was to meet with the agent and sign the necessary paperwork. What's more, he wanted me to play the character based on me, a proposition that sent me soaring into his arms.

Soon, we were in the bedroom, arms and legs and privates entangled in an octopusical display of sexual dexterity. Fletcher's newfound success had altered him, and our lovemaking was passionate and tender. I achieved orgasm for the first and second and third times in months.

Right before Fletcher's moment of climax, he stared into my eyes.

"I will always love you, Karen Jamey," he said.

His eyes rolled back into his head and he let out a guttural moan, on the verge of ecstasy.

Just as Fletcher's penis erupted in volcanic ecstasy, the bedroom door flung open. Tony looked at Fletcher. Fletcher looked at Tony. Without hesitation, Tony reached into his suit coat, pulled out a gun and fired three shots into Fletcher's body. Fletcher was knocked off of me, across the bed and onto the floor. Completely involuntarily, my muscles contracted, sending a tremendous orgasm through my body that made me scream with a divine combination of absolute pleasure and horror.

I scrambled furiously for the sheets in an attempt to cover up. I have always found it odd how, when a lover shoots another lover from atop your body while in the heat of passion, your first impulse is to cover up your nakedness. Such was my experience, at any rate. Body thus covered, I focused my attention on Tony, who stood stock still in the doorway. He wore no expression on his face, and his body betrayed no emotion.

"Tony, I ..." I began, my mind scrambling to come up with an excuse.

He slowly lowered his hand, dropped his pistol to the ground, then turned and walked to the living room.

I tossed on a bathrobe and ran out behind him. He was seated in a chair in the front room, mumbling something into the telephone. I sat on the floor at his feet and waited until he hung up.

"Frankie's coming over to take care of this," he said, with no emotion. "I don't know who that piece of shit was and I don't give a damn. In the morning, I'm taking you to the airport, and you're going to fly to Guatemala to lay low for awhile. The Commander will arrange someplace for you to stay. After that, I never want to hear from you again. As of this moment, you are dead to me."

"But, Tony," I pleaded, tears welling in my eyes, "this is my father's house. I can't just leave to Guatemala."

Tony lashed his meaty palm through the air and gave me a smack that sent me reeling against the floor. My cheek lit up with pain like it was being attacked by a herd of fire ants. I lay where I landed, sobbing; not from the pain, but from the wreck I had made of my life. Not one year before, I had been an ugly, boring waitress at Mr. Friendlier's, dreaming of fame and jumping around like a fat little jackass when the new issue of *Photoplay* arrived on the newsstands. Now, just look at me. Accessory to murder. Adulteress. Moll. And only two months shy of my 17th birthday.

But then, through the darkness, a light shone. Maybe Guatemala would be just the thing for me to break this cycle of sin in which I had imprisoned myself. A tropical vacation on an island paradise might be just what the doctor ordered. I could get my head together, find myself, and come back to America, better than ever. I could cleanse myself in the warm ocean waters and return to the States a new woman, filled with the youthful spirit that had been drained from my body over the months prior.

And maybe while I was down there, I could come up with a way to get Tony killed.

Chapter Thirteen

Guatemala, My Guatemala

The next morning, Tony drove me silently to an airstrip outside of Los Angeles and I stepped aboard an airplane for the first time in my life. Tony was owed a favor by a man who had a financial interest in Boeing, and they had been running test flights of a brand new luxury airplane called the Stratoliner. I was to be among the first passengers.

I would just as soon the memories of that trip were chemically erased from my mind. Science had not quite gotten the hang of commercial flight yet, and the trip to Guatemala was a stomach churning terror ride across the unfriendly skies. Still, the interior design was most luxurious, and when I wasn't screaming in fear or vomiting, I was skipping up and down the carpeted aisles of an aircraft made just for me.

The first thing I learned upon landing in Guatemala was that it isn't an island, nor was it the sort of tropical paradise I had imagined. A harsh rain shook the cabin as we descended and continued as the plane door opened to reveal my new hometown. From where I was standing, I could not see much of a town at all, although, to be fair, visibility was rather poor.

The Commander met me at the plane. I was so happy to be on solid ground again and to see a friendly face that I rushed into his arms. He let out a jovial laugh. "Ahh, little Karen," he said, in his exotic accent.

"So nice to be seeing you. Come with me, I will show you at your new home."

The Commander's limousine took us from the airport through the rough-and-tumble town of Guatemala City. I was terrified. Here I was, a young girl in a strange country, far from my family, on the run from a murder charge, and the only friend I had was a 50 year-old military commander. Everything had happened so quickly my brain hadn't been able to process the weight of my sudden exile.

"Karen," the Commander said, quietly," I worry about you. You know why I worry? I worry, because you are here in Guatemala, when you should be shaking your skirt and playing hoppity-jacks with the other girls. You are a beautiful young woman, Karen, but you are not so tough. I knew all along that you would be stepping into trouble with a man like Tony Tarantella."

"But I thought Tony was your friend," I responded.

The Commander laughed.

"A man in my position cannot afford to have friends, little Karen. A friend one day is an enemy the next. No, little Karen, people like me have business associates. Tony Tarantella is a business associate, and a valuable one. But he is not a friend. Never mistake the two."

"I see," I said. "Well, then, what am I?"

Tony laughed.

"You are a favor."

I nodded. Painful as it may be to be thought of as nothing more than a favor, at least the Commander was honest.

"But don't let this hurt you, little Karen," he said. "You will enjoy your time here with me, and I am looking forward to spending time with you, away from my business associate. Perhaps when you leave, I will call you friend."

"And I'll call you Daddy," I said suggestively, licking my lips.

"I'm sorry, my English is not so good," he replied with furrowed brow.

I turned away from him as we pulled into the guard station of the sprawling government complex. References checked, the guards opened up two enormous gates and we drove in. As the gates swung open, the rain suddenly stopped, the clouds parted, and the sun blazed down upon the opulent palace of President Jorge Ubico.

"The president is in," the Commander said.

"How do you know?" I asked.

"Because the sun is shining," he answered, simply.

We drove up to a large building next door to the capital. Men in military fatigues with ominous-looking guns strapped to their shoulders rushed forward from their posts in front of the building to carry my luggage. We stepped out of the car. The Commander shouted to the men in Spanish. The men saluted and stood in place, my luggage in their hands. I smiled and nodded in what I imagined to be a regal fashion. For all these men knew, I was an American princess in Guatemala on a diplomatic mission.

Once inside, the Commander led us up a giant, winding staircase to the third floor. The guest floor, he explained, held thirteen suites, complete with private bathrooms, kitchens, bedrooms, living rooms and studies. My suite was at the end of the hall. And what a suite it was! As we stepped into the living room, I gasped at the sheer opulence surrounding me. The curtains alone looked as though they cost more than my entire house back in Los Angeles. Classic paintings adorned the walls, and all of the furniture was of the highest quality. Tony had taken me to some fancy places, but nothing quite as extravagant as this.

The soldiers set my bags down, saluted the Commander, and left the room.

"I have one other thing to tell you, my dear Karen," the Commander said.

This was it, I imagined. Time for me to start paying off the favor. Well, such is my life, I thought, and began unbuttoning my shirt.

The Commander looked at me quizzically.

"Karen, please, show some modesty," he said. "Women do not behave the same way in Guatemala as they do in the United States."

"But I thought ..." I began.

"Mulgar!" the Commander barked.

"I'm sorry, I don't speak Spanish," I answered.

A tiny man with dark brown skin waddled into the room.

"This is Mulgar," the Commander said. "He will be your guardian in Guatemala. Please, do not go anywhere without him. A pretty girl like yourself could run into some trouble if caught wandering the streets alone."

I took a look at Mulgar. He couldn't have been more than three and a half feet tall. He had a large head and enormous ears that looked decidedly out of place on his small, rail-thin body. His face betrayed no hint of emotion, and there was a certain blankness in his eyes, like that of a very solemn, very intense baby. Although I had my doubts that he would be able to save me in a time of crisis, there was something imminently trustworthy and affable about this strange little man.

"No one will bother you if you are with Mulgar," the Commander assured. "The people of Guatemala know that he is with me."

"Does he speak any English?" I asked.

"He does not speak often, but he understands all."

Mulgar nodded.

The Commander kissed me on the forehead and left the room. Mulgar and I stared at one another.

"Hello, Mulgar," I said.

Mulgar nodded.

"I'm going to unpack now," I said.

Mulgar nodded.

"Could I have some time alone?" I asked him.

He nodded and left the room.

After I unpacked, I lay down on the bed and closed my eyes. I hadn't slept much the night before, what with my boyfriend brutally murdering my ex-boyfriend in front of me. Much as you might feel prepared for it, that's a hard image to shake. In those days, we didn't have the luxury of video games and action movies to desensitize us to violence. Our violence was real and, I like to think, more noble. Nowadays, you can barely walk down the streets in a new pair of athletic shoes without getting blasted to bits by some youngster with a Howitzer.

When I awoke, it was dark outside.

I opened the door to the hallway and peered out. Mulgar sat in a chair to the right of the doorway. When I opened the door, he snapped to attention.

"Hola, Mulgar," I said.

He nodded.

"Is anything happening around here, Mulgar?" I asked. "I could really use a drink."

Mulgar nodded, and waddled past me into the bedroom. He walked to the closet and paused in consideration. Finally, he grabbed one of my most flattering dresses from the rack, a lovely red and black Gilbert Adrian number that Tony bought for me. Mulgar motioned for me to put it on and turned his back.

I slipped out of my ugly old traveling gown and into the dress.

"Okay," I said.

Mulgar turned back around, looked me up and down, and nodded. He gently grabbed my hand with his tiny paw and led me across the room to the triple-mirrored makeup table that sat against the right wall. I sat down in the revolving chair. Mulgar pulled a stepstool over from near the window, hopped atop it, and got down to business. Grasping a comb between his teeth, he began working his lithe hands through my hair like a man possessed. In the midst of styling, I heard him utter his first word,

"Cream."

His spoke like a flower might speak if it had the ability to do so, poofing its sweet nectar into the air. The word lilted upon the wind and faded into nothingness, making me question whether or not it had ever been said in the first place.

"Cream?" I asked.

He pointed to a can sitting on the table. I handed it to him. He took off the top and worked its contents through my hair. He whipped the chair around and began work on my bangs. His face held a look of quiet concentration. Finally satisfied, he gave my head a light pat and spun me back around to see myself in the mirror.

"Mulgar," I gasped, "you're a genius."

Armed with a 35-cent bottle of hair cream and a pocket comb, Mulgar had done a finer job with my hair than any of the overpriced stylists in Hollywood. I barely recognized the gorgeous and vivacious woman staring back at me from the mirror.

"I look so ... glamorous," I said.

Mulgar leapt from the stepstool and waddled over to the dresser. Standing on tiptoes, he reached up to the top of the dresser and grabbed a small box that I had not noticed earlier. He brought it over to the makeup table and handed the box to me.

Tied to the top of the box with ribbon was a gift card. It read, "Enjoy this gift from your friend, the Commander. Please meet me in the State Room at 2100 hours."

I lifted the top off and peeked inside to find a dazzling diamond choker blazing back at me. I have never been very impressed with jewels. To me, there is no more beauty in a diamond than in a tree or a really nice rock. A diamond, perhaps, has hung around inside the earth a lot longer, but so have those giant toxic cockroaches they're always talking about, and I certainly would not want to wear one of those things on my neck. But, I know when someone has gone to trouble for me, so I made the appropriate "oohs" and "aahs" and instructed Mulgar to help me put on the necklace. He did, then handed me my gloves, shoes, and handbag. Outfit complete, I rose to my feet and followed Mulgar to the State Room on the first floor of the building.

As Mulgar and I slowly walked through the open doors of the State Room, the assembled crowd rose to their feet and applauded. I leaned down to Mulgar. "Are they applauding me?" I asked. He nodded. "Why?" I asked. He shrugged his shoulders.

The Commander walked through the crowd and up to me, beaming.

"Karen!" he said, jovially. "You are so beautiful!"

"Thank you," I said, "and thank you for the necklace. It's simply gorgeous."

He leaned in close to my ear.

"I told them you are an American movie star," he whispered. "And that you are researching life in Guatemala for a film role."

I smiled. It was the role I was born to play.

I shall cherish the memory of that first night in Guatemala as long as I live. Guatemalans, I discovered are quite a warm and generous people. During dinner, I was seated at a long banquet table at the front of the room, next to the lovely daughter of the General Jorge Ponce Vaides.

"What movies have you been in, Karen?" the daughter asked, in flawless English.

I held my head up, eyelids half closed, as I imagined a movie star might.

"Don't you know, dear?" I asked. "I was Daphne in *Hot Money!*"

"Ohhhh," the daughter replied, impressed. She turned to the person next to her and said something in Spanish. The woman listened with wide eyes and nodded her head to me in respect. She mumbled in Spanish back to the daughter.

"She says you were brilliant," the daughter said to me.

I gave her a Queenly nod, lids still at half mast.

"Charmed," I said.

As the dinner progressed, I began to find my character. I was a brilliant and beloved American actress, the acclaimed star of the box office smash *Hot Money!* The role I was researching was for a film called *In the Throes of a Dream,* a tender love story set in Guatemala against the backdrop of the Great Depression. I was to play Rosario Valdez, a simple coffee bean picker who falls in love with the President of the United Fruit Company. It was, at heart, a *Romeo and Juliet* story, as is every great love story that has ever been told. Including most of those other Shakespeare plays.

I met many wonderful people and danced the night away. Periodically, I would check back in with the Commander, who appeared to be having a gay old time. He spent the night draped on the arm of President Ubico, whispering pleasantries into the old man's ear.

When the Commander finally stepped away, President Ubico waved me over. I walked to his seat and curtsied. He motioned for me to sit down.

"Miss Jamey, let me be the first to tell you that you are a welcome presence in our country," he said.

I blushed.

"Thank you very much, Mr. President," I said. "And thank you for allowing me to stay here."

The President leaned closer and whispered to me conspiratorially.

"Tell me, Karen," he asked, "how well do you know the Commander?"

"The Commander is a dear friend," I lied.

"I see," the President nodded. "And tell me, Karen, do you think he is a loyal man?"

"Oh, yes," I answered. "He has a great admiration for you."

The president smiled. He slowly leaned back in his seat.

"Very good, Karen," he said.

I felt a hand on my shoulder. I turned my head to see the Commander standing behind me. When I glanced up at his face, I felt a chill run through me. His brows were furrowed and his lips pursed in an expression that I could not quite place. It was almost a look of ... jealousy.

"And what were you two discussing?" he asked.

"I ... I was just telling the President how happy I am to be here, and how grateful you are to be working for him," I stammered.

The Commander broke into a wide smile.

"Very good, Karen," he said. "Very good."

I was feeling tired and slightly unsettled, so I politely excused myself. From out of nowhere, Mulgar appeared to lead me back to the room.

I was greeted with another round of applause as I left the room. This time, I didn't need to ask Mulgar why they were clapping. I had earned this applause. It was the finest acting job of my career.

I went to sleep that night a fugitive from the law. I awoke the next morning a Guatemalan celebrity.

Chapter Fourteen
Rebel, Rebel

I woke up early, refreshed and eager to have a look around my new city. Mulgar was at the door the minute I stepped out, holding aloft a newspaper with my name and picture splashed across the front page.

"What does it say? What does it say?" I asked Mulgar, eagerly

He shook his head.

"No? Oh, do read it to me Mulgar," I pleaded.

He shook his head again. From inside his jacket, he produced a Spanish-English dictionary and handed it to me.

I rolled my eyes.

"You're an impossible little man, you know that?"

Mulgar nodded.

I sat down at the breakfast table with the dictionary and newspaper and began to translate. The headline read, "*Hot Money!* Star Comes to Guatemala." According to the article, I was the brightest up-and-coming actress in Hollywood, and *In the Throes of a Dream* was expected to top all box office records. Reportedly, the fabulous Errol Flynn was to play my love interest.

I was ecstatic until I remembered that the film didn't exist and I was supposed to be lying low. I was caught in the midst of the dilemma that would affect me many times later in life. More than anything, I desired recognition, but here I was, receiving it at the most inopportune time for something I did not even do. The problem is universal, I'm sure. A man puts his heart and soul into coaching a Little League team, but what does he finally become known for? Child molestation.

I sent Mulgar off to find the Commander, who repaired to my bedroom quickly.

"This is an outrage!" he screamed, as he walked in the door. "No one is to know you are here! Who tells these people these stories?"

"The only person I spoke to was the daughter of General Vaides," I said.

"Ponce!" the Commander shouted, throwing his finger in the air. "I should have known this. He causes me trouble, always. I am reporting to the president at once this crime!"

The Commander stormed off to alert the president. I had a queasy feeling in the pit of my stomach that I was getting dragged into the middle of something that would come back to haunt me.

Nonetheless, it was a beautiful day, and I was determined to see the sights. Mulgar escorted me to a limousine that took us out of the gated government complex and into downtown Guatemala City.

We left the limo driver behind at the mouth of the crowded Guatemala shopping district. As soon as we stepped out of the car, all eyes were upon me. Whispers danced from mouth to mouth as I strode the bustling city streets. Here, I was a celebrity, and I stepped into the role with abandon. A benevolent smile emanated from my face as I held my body high above the dirty sidewalks.

The vibrant colors of real life shone brightly in Guatemala City. Everywhere around me, people went about their daily business with a passion and joy that is seldom seen among the over-educated parlor-dwellers of the United States. Here, a man rides aback a contented donkey! Thither, a beggar sips tequila and wonders at what might have been in a life spent chasing the bottle! The children play native games in flowing skirts, and a clever chicken entertains with magic tricks!

Mulgar led me through the vegetable stands and clothing tents to a seemingly abandoned store front. He knocked once, paused, then knocked again.

"Where are we going, Mulgar?" I asked.

He shrugged his shoulders.

The door opened a crack. A pair of eyes peered out from inside. Seeing Mulgar, the door opened wider. A solemn-looking man in a colorful outfit motioned us inside.

I hesitated at the threshold of the building. I had no plans for this day, besides enjoying a bit of the local culture, but apparently Mulgar had other notions. Now we were standing outside the kind of building I imagined Tony went to when he said he had to "take care of some business." Mulgar walked ahead, then turned to look into my eyes. His face said, "Trust me." I did have an unexplainable trust in the tiny brown scamp. I followed him in, and the door was shut behind me.

We stood inside a dimly-lit room with three men, all dressed in similarly colorful clothing. One of the men stepped forth. As he walked into the light that streamed through the window, my heart dropped into my stomach. He was absolutely breathtaking ... among the most gorgeous men I had ever or will ever see. A fiery passion burned in his deep brown eyes. He had a wiry yet muscular frame, every inch of which seemed to be working overtime to keep up with his intense mind. He wore a dapper, Clark Gable moustache across his upper lip, a moustache that I longed to have tickling my belly.

He moved in close to me and stared deep into my eyes. Then he grabbed my quivering hand, lifted it to his mouth, and planted a tender kiss upon it.

"Karen Jamey," he said softly. "I ... am Juan Banana."

"Juan Banana," I repeated.

"No, no," he said. "Juan BAH-na-na. The accent is on the first syllable. The voice gets softer as the name comes to a close, and by the time you reach the final syllable, I am but a memory."

"Juan BAH-na-na," I repeated.

"You are shivering, Karen," he whispered. "A woman so beautiful as yourself must never shiver. A woman so beautiful as yourself must be comfortable, always."

"Your voice," I whispered back. "It's like music."

Juan smiled softly.

"Come, Karen," he whispered. "Sit with me. Let us talk."

The two silent men pulled chairs up behind us. We sat. Juan held my hands in his as he stared into my eyes.

"When I saw you in the newspaper this morning, Karen, I knew I must speak with you. Before I begin, I want to be certain that I can trust you. Please tell me; how well do you know the Commander?"

"He is a friend of the man who sent me here."

Juan smiled.

"And this man is Tony Tarantella, the American gangster?"

"Yes," I answered, surprised.

Juan nodded.

"Yes, Karen Jamey, yes," he said. "And where does your allegiance lie?"

"Right now," I said, "to you and you alone."

Juan smiled, pleased with my answer.

"Good, Karen Jamey," he said. "Mulgar brought you here because he felt you could be trusted. Can you be trusted?"

"I can be trusted," I said. "Please trust me, Juan Banana. Trust me with all you have to offer."

"Very well," he replied. "Your friend, the Commander, is not the man he seems. As right-hand man to President Ubico, he is responsible for the deaths of many of my countrymen. I and my colleagues are fomenting a revolution against this regime, and I need you to help us. Would you help us, Karen Jamey?"

"Yes, Juan," I answered, thoroughly taken away by the moment. "I will do whatever it takes."

I listened intently as Juan launched into an explanation of the situation. President Ubico, it seems, ruled Guatemala with an iron fist. The United Fruit Company ruled the President. When the Great Depression hit in '29, Guatemala suffered a severe economic decline. United Fruit threatened to leave the country unless Ubico granted them enormous tax subsidies.

Meanwhile, the Commander, Ubico's right-hand man, was secretly traveling to the United States to arrange a deal between United Fruit and Tony Tarantella. Tony would import bananas from Guatemala through his underground network, thus avoiding the stiff importing and exporting fees that were applied to international trade. United Fruit paid 30% of what they would have paid in export fees to the Commander, who split the money between himself and Tony.

"That's what Tony does?" I asked. "He imports bananas?"

"Not just bananas, Karen," Juan answered, shaking his head. "Yellow gold."

"So what is my role in this mess?" I asked, puzzled.

"Ponce is angling for the Commander's position. He found out about the Commander's trips to Los Angeles, and he informed the President. Now, no one knows *why* the Commander has been making these trips, but Ponce is suspicious, and he has instilled these same suspicions in the President. If the President found out that the Commander was working in secret with United Fruit, he would have the Commander murdered.

"You, Karen Jamey, came at an extraordinarily opportune time for our dear Commander. The very day you arrived, the Commander was set to meet with Ubico to discuss the secret trips to Los Angeles. The Commander told the President that he has been meeting with Tarantella to arrange your visit to Guatemala. What is this, this project you are working on?"

"*In the Throes of a Dream.*"

"Yes. *Throw the Dream.* The Commander told Ubico that anticipation for this movie is extraordinarily high in America, and no one was to know that you are here. Ponce, of course, found this out, and he leaked the news to the press, with the hopes that the Americans will now come after the Commander."

"Good lord!" I exclaimed. "And how in the hell do you know all of this?"

"Tony Tarantella and the Commander both socialize with my sister. I believe you know her ... the good Countess D'arger."

"Countess D'arger is your sister? I thought she was Russian!"

"We are all brothers and sisters in the revolution, Karen," he said seriously.

"I always wondered how a Russian woman learned to make such smashing margaritas," I replied.

Juan continued on with some mumbo-jumbo about politics, but I had stopped listening. Here I was, caught up in a web of international intrigue, with nary an idea. It was all very exciting and dramatic, as life should be.

"How can I help?" I asked when he finally stopped speaking.

Juan smiled.

"We are going to bring this regime down from the inside, Karen. We have already infiltrated the military. If we can provoke a struggle between Ponce, Ubico, and the Commander, we can split their loyalists into factions and stage a coup. I need you to be my eyes and ears inside the regime. No one will suspect a thing of you."

"Juan, you do seem like a darling man, and I would love to help you," I said, "but how are we going to meet? It's difficult to keep a low profile when you're the most famous actress in Guatemala. It won't do for me to be cavorting around with revolutionaries."

"Do not worry," Juan replied, calmly. "Brother Mulgar will arrange everything."

Mulgar raised his fist in solidarity.

"Now, go, Karen Jamey," Juan said. "Go. We will meet again soon, under more comfortable conditions."

He kissed my hand again, and a tingle ran through my body. We would meet again under more comfortable conditions, all right. By that, I mean we would have sex.

That night, I called Daddy. It was a difficult call to make. Since he had left Los Angeles, essentially all of my communication with him had been based on fabrications. How could I ever tell him that his precious daughter, the one he had left so pure and carefree, had gone from stripper to adulteress to murder accessory to Communist revolutionary?

Instead, I told Daddy that I had accepted the lead in the Guatemalan production of the famous stage play *In the Throes of a Dream*. He was overjoyed to hear that my acting career was back on track.

"But Guatemala, Karen?" he asked. "Is that safe?"

"Oh yes," I said. "I'm safer here than in Los Angeles." On this point, I didn't have to lie.

"Well, I hope the house is okay," he said.

Shit. The house. I had forgotten about the house. For all I knew, Tony had turned it into a strip club.

Well, nothing I could do about it while in Guatemala. Daddy planned to remain in Baltimore for another two or three months, and I was hoping to be comfortably back in L.A. by that point. I was certain the details would work themselves out, and if they didn't, I would find a way to deal with it. After all, I'd managed to get along this far without ever thinking deeply about things.

Granpapa was doing well, according to Daddy. He was out of the wheelchair and speaking in complex sentences again. He was still in quite a bit of pain, but the doctors said that would subside as he continued his therapy. News about Granpapa always left me with a certain sense of humility. If this man could, at 60 years old, manage to snap back from a four year coma, I should be able to fix my insignificant problems. There is always a light at the end of the tunnel. For everyone who thinks that their problems are overwhelming, remember: somewhere in America there is a 60 year-old man with drool on his chin, trying to figure out which utensil to use for soup. This is the man you should look to for inspiration. Unless he never learned how to eat soup in the first place, in which case, there is probably something severely wrong with him.

That week, I established my regular routine. I woke up around noon and had Mulgar bring me breakfast in bed. Then I walked to the bar on the first floor of the palace and drank fruity Guatemalan drinks until 2:00. I would retire to my bedroom until 3:00, get lunch in bed, return to the bar until 7:00, then eat dinner in the State Room with Mulgar and whomever else happened to be lolling about. My fellow guests consisted mainly of foreign dignitaries and Guatemalan governmental figures. Naturally, I was an object of great fascination among these horny old men and an object of scorn among their hornier old wives.

I kept my ears open for information to bring to Juan Banana, with little success. All the locals wanted to talk about was my stupid movie. I was considering making something up, when, on my fifth day in the country, I finally overheard a conversation that guaranteed another meeting with the mysterious and delicious Juan Banana.

Mulgar and I were sitting alone, enjoying our dinner, when I heard the name Juan Banana slip across someone's lips at the next table. I glanced to my left to see the General locked in intense conversation with the President. The Commander was nowhere to be found. I looked at Mulgar to see if he was catching the conversation. He nodded to me. As the discussions in the State Room tended to be in Spanish, there was little I could do but hope that Mulgar's gigantic ears were on the case.

We returned to my room after dinner. Mulgar sat down immediately at the desk and began writing. When he was finished, he handed the note to me. I read it. It seemed the polite thing to do.

The General know that Juan Banana want revolt. He convince President that Commander work with Juan Banana. They find Juan hideout and they get him tomorrow night. Then they get Commander.

A chill ran through me as I read his words. The Commander was the only ally I had in Guatemala. If something happened to him, and if anyone discovered I'd interacted with Juan Banana, I could be in great danger. I thought to myself, "what would Rosario Valdez do in this situation?" She would be strong, I concluded. Much like the coffee beans she picked for a living, Rosario would be strong, honest, and hearty, with a slightly bitter aftertaste.

Just then, I heard the door open behind me. Thinking fast, I slid the paper into the top desk drawer, then turned around to see the Commander standing before me, a wide smile on his face.

"Karen!" he said, jovially. "I had not see you very much in here! I stop by to check how you do, my favorite lamb!"

I tried to catch Mulgar's eye, but he only stared straight ahead, unblinking. Mulgar would be no help to me now. The decision was mine to make alone.

"Commander," I began, "I think you should sit down."

"Is there a matter of something, Karen?" the Commander asked. "You are so pale."

"Commander," I replied, bluntly, "Mulgar and I have reason to believe that you're going to be killed."

The Commander sat in the chair next to the davenport, a worried expression on his face. I told him what we had overheard, leaving out the part about Juan Banana. Although the Commander and I were in the same boat, he did not need to know that I'd been mucking about in the engine room with the bootblack.

"This is a very serious thing, Karen," the Commander said. "I thank you for saying this thing to me. I think I maybe am not so safe, and maybe you are not so either. I think that maybe we get out from this place quick. I talk to Tony tonight, I find out what we are doing. You do not do nothing, do you understand? You stay here and I find you when I have plans. You will do this for me?"

"Yes, I will stay right here," I lied.

The Commander rose and saluted me.

"You are good, Karen Jamey," he said, before leaving. "You are a friend."

When we were certain that the Commander was at a safe distance, Mulgar and I took off. He led me out to the garage, where we climbed into a waiting car. The driver turned around and raised his fist in solidarity. We gave him the fist back, and off we drove into the Guatemalan City night.

I have been high many times in my life. I've done reefer, speed, acid, crank, cat, smack, and smork. I've gone goofy on goofballs, wacky on crack, and quazy on Quaaludes. I once sucked off a live baboon. But for my money, nothing beats the rush of charging through the streets of a foreign city on the eve of a revolution, knowing that you're mere minutes away from saving a man's life ... and hopefully screwing him blind.

We pulled up to headquarters and got out of the car. With a series of grunts, Mulgar instructed the driver to circle the block until we were ready to leave. Mulgar gave the secret knock, and I was welcomed in by Juan. Mulgar waited outside on guard duty.

"To what do I owe this pleasure?" Juan asked when we were safely ensconced inside the office. His eyes smoldered through me like a cigarette through a Halston top.

"You're going to die," I blurted out.

Juan smiled. "We are all going to die, Karen," he said. "But will we die as cowards? Or as men? Or as women, who can also be quite brave?"

I shook my head. "No, Juan, you're going to die tomorrow. The

President has it in for you and he knows where you live."

If Juan had any fear, he didn't show it. He kept his eyes focused intently on me as he walked backwards to the stove, lit a burner, and placed a tea kettle on top.

"You must tell me all about it," he said. "But first, please, join me in a cup of tea."

"I'd love to, Juan," I said, "but I don't know if we'll fit in those tiny teacups."

Juan laughed.

"Your wit, like your beauty, knows no bounds," he said.

I took a seat on the cot and crossed my legs seductively. Juan remained standing by the stove. We stared at one another as we waited for the tea to boil. When the whistle of the tea kettle pierced the air, he grabbed the handle and poured us two cups, never removing his eyes from mine. He walked across the room to the cot, leaned forward, and placed a cup in my hand.

"Drink, Karen," he whispered. "Drink and make merry."

I brought the steaming tea to my lips and blew softly upon its surface.

"Yes," Juan whispered, "blow, my darling. Cool it down before you drink it, yes."

I raised the glass to my mouth and took a small sip. I let out a squeak of surprise as the scalding hot liquid burned my tongue.

"No!" Juan shouted. He suddenly stood, grabbed the cup out of my hands, and flung it against the wall. "I will not allow this tea to mock you with its heat! It and its confidante, the cup, will rot in eternal Hell!

"Never again, Karen," he continued, tenderly. "Never again shall you experience pain in the shack of Juan Banana."

With that, he took my head in his hands and planted a soft, passionate kiss upon my lips. I grabbed him around the waist and pulled him on top of me.

"Now I will show you how communists make love," he whispered.

And boy, did he ever. Communists make love in basically the same way as non-communists; by putting their penises into vaginas. But there was a whole mess of other things thrown in there that sure felt nice.

We lay on his cot afterwards, naked, smoking tobacco wrapped in palm leaves. It was a balmy evening and we were both sweaty from our roll in the hay. Juan had his arm around me, his hand cupping my breast.

"Now, tell me, Karen," Juan said. "How do you mean I will die?"

As I related the details of the evening, Juan listened intently, a look of concentration on his face. When I was finished, he continued staring at the ceiling, as if searching for meaning in the cracked plaster that hung above his head.

"Karen," he said, finally, "there is something I must tell you."

A loud knock on the door suddenly blasted through the silence. Juan bolted up in bed. We both raced feverishly to get dressed. Just as I was pulling up the zipper on my dress, the door flung open and in walked the Commander.

The Commander stared at me with a look of disgust as I rose from the bed and frantically attempted to smooth my disheveled hair. He looked to Juan, who regarded him with a steely gaze. My legs were paralyzed by fear.

Juan broke the silence.

"Hello, Father," he spat.

I turned to Juan, puzzled. He and the Commander stared at each other, like two angry dogs, circling their territory. Only they weren't circling, they were just standing there, and neither of them looked much like dogs.

"I tell you not to leave, Karen," the Commander finally said slowly, his eyes still fastened on Juan. "And here I find you with this, this infidel. This is not a child game. This is serious."

"Leave her alone," Juan said.

"Leave her alone?" the Commander said, his voice rising. "Leave her alone? It is you who must leave her alone!"

He turned to me.

"We have a plane waiting at the airport to take us to Los Angeles, Karen," he said. "We must go now, or we will both die."

"Don't listen to him, Karen," Juan said. "Stay with me. I know where we can go. We will win this revolution and you will stay and be my wife."

I looked from man to man. Man and man looked from man to man and at me. I took a deep breath and turned to Juan.

"Did you just call him 'father'?" I asked.

"Dammit, Karen!" shouted the Commander. "We must leave now!"

"Stay, Karen," Juan pleaded. "Together, we will lead the country to peace and prosperity."

I looked behind the Commander, at Mulgar, for a hint as to what to do. Mulgar shrugged. It was all in my hands, now. I could leave with the Commander, back to Los Angeles where I was potentially wanted as an accessory to murder. Or, I could stay in Guatemala and take my chances on the revolution, with the hopes of becoming the glamorous first lady of the new president, or dictator, or whatever it is they have in communist countries.

I knew what I had to do. I closed my eyes, held out my hand, and leapt into the void.

Chapter Fifteen

The Void

What, do you think I'm a fucking idiot? I high-tailed it out of that shit-hole the first chance I got. Don't get me wrong, darling, Juan Banana was gorgeous, and one Hell of a cocksman, but I could never live in a country where they didn't even have brie.

The Commander, Mulgar, and I took a private plane back to the States. The return trip was not quite as trying as my original trip out to Guatemala, perhaps because I had such lovely gentlemen to keep me company. Mulgar was positively beaming with the excitement of being on a plane. You would think the little monkey had died and gone to heaven, the way he scampered back and forth between the seats. For all his troubles, the Commander was in jovial spirits. He nattered on about the new life he was going to forge in America, far away from the backstabbers and position-grubbers and phonies that populated his workaday world. I didn't have the heart to remind him that we were going to Hollywood.

We touched down early the next evening. As I stepped off the plane, I was hit with the welcoming smell of jasmine. My soul rejoiced to be back in my home country. I breathed in the delicious American air and made a promise to myself that the next time I left the country, it would be on my terms.

The Commander had been so kind in saving my life that I invited him to stay with me until he could find his own place. I couldn't really toss Mulgar out on the street after we'd been through so much together, so I let him tag along, as well. We were a motley crew, all right. When I think of it, I am reminded of that old joke: an actress, a dictator, and a dwarf walk into a bar. I don't remember how the rest of it goes, but I seem to recall that it was quite amusing.

I was tentative about what to expect when we pulled into the driveway, but once we got inside, I was pleased to see that everything appeared to be shipshape. Nary a trace of murder was to be found anywhere in the house. All of the nasty bits had been scrubbed and painted away in my bedroom. At first, I didn't think that I would be able to fall asleep at the crime scene, but then I remembered I was dreadfully tired. I threw some blankets out at my gentlemen friends and settled into a pleasant sleep.

The next day I awoke to find Mulgar looming over me. I jumped up in shock.

"Good lord, Mulgar!" I shouted. "You could have given me a heart attack!"

Mulgar pointed toward the door.

I released a deep sigh.

"You're an insufferable little man," I said. "I'm not going out there until you tell me why you're pointing like that."

Mulgar's face remained fixed in its usual blank expression. He curled his arm up to his chest and threw his finger out again, pointing toward the doorway.

"Just one word, Mulgar," I said. "For me?"

"Tony," he finally said.

My blood ran cold, as I was suddenly reminded of the high stakes venture in which I had become embroiled. Nonetheless, I was a trooper, and I knew that I would have to see Tony eventually. I threw on a bathrobe and walked out into the living room.

Tony and the Commander were sitting on the davenport, sipping coffee. When I walked in the room, Tony rose from the sofa. He held his arms out to me, an idiot smile beaming from his gorilla face.

"There's my gal," Tony said.

I turned away from his embrace and took a seat in the rocking chair.

"Good morning, Commander," I said.

Tony dropped his arms and sat back down on the sofa.

"The Commander tells me you had quite a little adventure down in Guatemala," Tony said. He let out a small chuckle and shook his head. "Boy, Karen, ya' sure do manage to get yourself into some sticky situations."

"Mulgar! Coffee!" I barked.

"Anyway," Tony continued, "I just stopped by to let ya' know that everything is all taken care of. Your boyfriend Fletcher disappeared and no one cared. Honestly, I've killed street scum that left behind more loved ones than that prick."

I shot Tony a withering glance.

"He wasn't a prick, Tony," I spat. "He was a good man. Sure, he hit the bottle too hard, and yeah, he liked to sleep with little girls, but he was a decent man at heart. Not like you, you, you murderer!"

Tony chuckled.

"She's a pip, ain't she?" he asked the Commander.

"The knees of the bee," the Commander replied.

Tony rose from the sofa and put on his coat. The Commander did the same. When they were all suited up, Tony turned to me.

"You've got one coming," Tony said, mysteriously. "And it'll come. It might not come for years. But let me make one thing very clear, Karen Jamey. You do not fuck with Tony Tarantella and get away with it."

"Well, we'll just see about that, won't we?" I asked.

"We certainly will," he answered, then turning to the Commander, "I'll meet you in the car."

The Commander stepped forward and grasped my hands in his.

"Karen, I thank you for letting me stay in this place. I now will go with Tony, and he helps me find some other place. For saving me, I give you a present. You may have Mulgar."

"You're giving me Mulgar?" I asked, incredulous.

I felt a tug on my sleeve. Mulgar stood next to me, extending a coffee mug. I took the cup from him and took a sip. The little freak sure could make a damn good cup of coffee.

"Do you hear that, Mulgar?" I asked. "The Commander is giving you to me."

Mulgar nodded.

"Well, thanks, I guess," I said.

The Commander smiled, pleased.

I choked back tears as he walked out the door. An era of my life was over, and a new one was just beginning. I looked down at the calm, emotionless little man who stood beside me. He looked back at me with enormous puppy dog eyes. Truth be told, I was happy to hear that he'd be sticking around.

"Mulgar," I began.

He stared at me expectantly.

"Go clean my room."

Chapter Sixteen

A New Life

It is now the fall of 1939. Or, rather, it was then, at the time that I'm describing. In reality we are now somewhere in the aughts, or, heaven forbid, the traughts, should my words or civilization last that long.

It was a period of great change for both myself and the world. In the world, there were some things happening in Europe and China that had something to do with World War II. In America, of course, the big news was that *Gone With the Wind* was to begin shooting soon, and the pivotal role of Scarlett O' Hara had not yet been filled.

The events of that magically terrible summer left me with a renewed sense of purpose. Life was short, I realized, and I had to grab my opportunities before they slipped away forever. I didn't know it then, but life isn't really that short. It goes on for quite some time. You struggle and suffer and sometimes succeed, and then everyone you know dies and you wind up in an old folks home, living with a babbling idiot named Myrna and her filthy cat, Costco. Or so I've heard.

On November 27 1939, Mulgar and I met with a new agent, Pauly Auskie. Pauly's office was a noticeable improvement over Jack Scallinger's. Where Jack had a cot, Pauly had a couch, and where Jack had his four walls, Pauly had space, because the walls of his office were much further apart.

Pauly rose and greeted us warmly. He was a dapper looking man with dark hair and a pencil-thin moustache, as was the style at the time. His pin-striped suit looked like it cost a pretty penny, and whereas Jack's clothes always hung loosely on his wiry frame, Pauly's suit was neatly tailored.

Pauly showed us to the couch and took a seat behind his desk. He stared at me for a moment silently, taking in the entire picture. Mulgar sat quietly next to me, his tiny legs dangling awkwardly above the floor.

"Well, Karen," Pauly finally said, "you certainly have the looks to be a star."

I blushed. It was a false blush. I knew I was gorgeous.

"Thank you, Mr. Auskie," I said. "I owe it all to Mulgar. He's my stylist."

"Oh, come now," Pauly said, sincerely. "He did a fine job with your hair and your makeup. But God gave you those really great tits."

I blushed. This time, it was real.

"Tell me, Karen, how are your chops?"

"Very nice," I said, opening my mouth and gnashing my teeth. "See?"

Pauly shook his head. "Not your choppers, your chops. Your skills. Can you buffalo an audience into believing in you? Can you make a monkey weep? The Auskie Agency doesn't invest in pretty faces alone. Pretty faces are a dime a dozen. Tits like that are somewhat rarer, but costumers can work wonders with wire and sculpting clay. I need to be convinced you're worth my time. Give it to me straight, Sally. How much butter you got on that toast?"

"I assure you, Mr. Auskie," I said "I've got enough butter for my toast and yours."

"I like the way you talk," Pauly said. "But can you dance?"

I stood up from my chair and launched into the tap solo from the opening number of *Hot Money!* The sun was shining, and I was on fire. I ended the two-minute routine standing atop Pauly's desk, panting and staring down at him. Mulgar clapped politely from the couch while Pauly let out a low whistle.

"You're a hoofer, that's for sure," he murmured. "But what I'm looking for is a triple threat. Gimme a little taste of those pipes."

I blasted through the opening verse of "O! Dilly-o' Ka-dilly Ay," a popular number at the time. The closing note had Pauly and Mulgar on their feet with excitement.

"You think that's good?" I asked, jumping off the desk. "Take a listen to this."

I turned my back to Pauly and took a moment to compose myself, then turned around again to face him. Pauly jumped back slightly in reaction to my startling transformation; from Karen Jamey to Cat Parsons in *The Trinidadian*.

"What is the price of a kiss?" I cried to the air. "For me, it has cost a lifetime from the ones I love, a lifetime under the thumb of a most cruel taskmaster called fate. But I am back now, Inigo, and a kiss will never again take me away, lest it be the heavenly kiss of Jesus, showing me off to that beautiful land above the mountains. Can you hear the doves cooing, Inigo? It is for you they coo, and you alone. Now remove your heavy coat and come sit by the fire, my darling, and together we shall find a kiss that is affordable to us both."

I collapsed to the floor in a heap as Pauly and Mulgar went wild with applause. They gathered on both sides of me and helped me to my feet. Pauly handed me a handkerchief that was damp with his own tears.

"That was beautiful, kid, absolutely beautiful," Pauly said. "With your talent, and my connections, we're going all the way to the top."

I signed a five-year contract that very day at a more reasonable and traditional 90/10 split. Mulgar and I left the office with the promise of major auditions in our near future. Everything was looking up as we drove through the streets of Hollywood, singing along to "A-Tisket, A-Tasket" on the Motorola radio. Mulgar did not actually sing, of course, but he bopped his head along to the beat, happier and more at home than he had been in the entire time I'd known him. I treated him to a banana split at Mr. Friendlier's in celebration.

Capping off the perfect day, we arrived at home to find Daddy's car in the driveway.

I rushed inside and flew into Daddy's arms, Mulgar following close behind.

"Oh, Daddy!" I squealed. "You're home, you're home, you're home!"

Daddy laughed and gave me a warm embrace.

"I missed you so, my darling," he said.

"I missed you, too, Daddy," I said, snuggling into his chest.

Daddy's eye happened to fall on Mulgar, who stood beside me, smiling up expectantly.

"Say, Karen?" he whispered. "Who's the little brown man?"

I pulled away from Daddy and looked him in the eye.

"He was a gift from the Commander of the Armed Services of Guatemala. He's my personal assistant, and I love him. Can we keep him, Daddy? Please?"

Daddy looked at Mulgar suspiciously.

"Karen," he said to me. "I don't think it's legal to just keep people."

"Oh, but he's not here against his will, Daddy," I said. "You're here by choice, aren't you, Mulgar?"

Mulgar nodded his head vigorously.

"Well," Daddy relented, "now that Granpapa's here, we will need someone to assist him. Maybe we can put your little friend on the payroll."

I jumped away from Daddy and clapped my hands to my face in excitement.

"Granpapa's here?" I asked. "Where? Oh, where?"

"I'm right here, Karen," he said.

I looked behind Daddy to see Granpapa leaning against the arch between the living room and the dining room. He looked somewhat older and worse for the wear, but behind his eyes I could see the mischievous spirit of the old Nip I knew. My eyes welled up in tears as I rushed into his arms and planted a loving kiss on his cheek.

That night, the four of us got to know each other again, and it was lovely. We grilled steaks on the veranda and drank Maryland wine and caught up on the last few months of our lives ... or in my case, the falsified version of the last few months. Save for a slight lisp, Granpapa seemed good as new, although still somewhat saddened to be living without Granny. Granpapa took an instant liking to Mulgar, and at the end of the evening, Daddy graciously welcomed the little scamp into our family.

I went to sleep that evening on top of the world. I was awarded a gift most precious, a gift that few of us are lucky enough to receive in our lifetimes. With the return of Daddy and Granpapa, I was given back my youth. Months of pretending to be an adult melted away. I fell asleep at peace, clutching my beloved stuffed donkey, Emipeedle, to my chest.

A few days later, I received an exuberant phone call from Pauly Auskie.

"Karen," he said, trying to contain his excitement, "I have some amazing news. I showed your headshot to a friend at MGM, and he wants you to come in and test for *Gone with the Wind*."

I screamed into the telephone receiver. Mulgar heard me screaming and started screaming himself.

"What in the world are you screaming about?" Granpapa asked him.

Mulgar shrugged his shoulders and continued screaming.

"That was my agent!" I shouted, hanging up the phone. "I'm testing for Scarlett O' Hara!"

Granpapa clapped his hands and joined in the screaming. Just then, Daddy returned home from a job interview to find his house overrun by a group of shrieking jackasses. I broke the news and he joined us, hopping around the living room and caterwauling like a bunch of gay fools.

The day of the screen test, I felt confident, relaxed, and ready to step into my rightful place in cinematic history. Mulgar went the extra mile with my hair and makeup that morning, giving my bouffant an alluring flip that was certain to knock the pants off of the casting agents.

Mulgar and I arrived on the MGM lot and showed our I.D.s to the guard at the gate. It was a thrilling moment ... the first time I ever set foot on the most famous studio lot in the world. Mulgar was equally excited, craning his neck and peering around avidly like a horny little boy at a booby circus.

One other actress sat in the waiting room, going over her sides. I got my sides from the attendant and sat down across from the other actress. Mulgar and I shared an amused glance at the other actress's appearance. She was dressed entirely in period clothes, an enormous hoop skirt forcing her to perch awkwardly on the end of her seat. I crossed my legs and began reading my sides. If this ninny was my strongest competition, I had this one in the bag.

I was called in first. I shared a phony smile with the other actress and a mumbled, "Good luck."

Three stone-faced judges sat across from me in the audition room. A camera whirred away in the corner. I took my chair across from the casting agents and launched into my sides. I poured my heart into that audition, and by the end of my speech, there wasn't a dry eye in the house. The agents thanked me sincerely and told me they'd be in touch soon.

I left the room and they called in the other actress, a no-talent foreign hack named Vivien Leigh.

As near as I can figure, Vivien Leigh must really know how to suck a great cock. Because I stayed behind and listened to that audition, and let me tell you, her performance did not hold a candle to mine. But I was green; I didn't know how to work the politics. I didn't realize that the audition was just the first step in the process. Vivien had a real leg up on me in that regard, as she was already playing a bit part in the film and had easy access to George Cukor, the director. While I went home and spent the rest of the day playing Tiddly-Pigs with Mulgar on the veranda, Vivien got straight to work, sucking and fucking her way through the cast and crew. But I'm not bitter, and I wish Ms. Leigh all the luck in the world should she ever return from the dead.

The audition was not a complete waste of time, fortunately. I may not have secured the lead in the most popular and award-winning film of all time, but I came in a close second. A mere two days after the audition, MGM called me to let me know that, although that snooty cunt Vivien Leigh would be stealing the role that was really supposed to go to me, another director was so impressed with my screen test that he would like me to play the role of Madge Slippery, the scrappy young sister of a female prospector in Werner Von Growlers' new film, *The Slippery Girls of Grizzly Gulch.*

Chapter Seventeen

Slippery When Wet

That Christmas season was the happiest of my life. Between Granpapa, Daddy, and Mulgar, I felt like I had a real family again. We would gather in the living room every night, listening to our favorite radio programs and holding hands. Daddy and Granpapa liked the mystery shows like *Dick Giant,* but Mulgar and I loved the quiz shows. Mulgar would get so excited when he knew the answers he'd pee his pants. This would make Granpapa pee his pants, which would send me and Daddy into hysterics, and soon we'd all be laughing and peeing and having a jolly time.

When away from the confines of his impoverished country, Mulgar turned out to be a ball of fun, and he had a laugh that was absolutely infectious. He was quite the little performer, too; Granpapa taught him all the old Nip n' Tuck routines, and they would sometimes put on funny hats and perform them for a rapturous audience of Daddy and me. Mulgar's silent nature added an unexpected twist to the routines, which Granpapa enjoyed. He felt like he was creating again, coming up with new complications based on Mulgar's inefficiencies. Lest you think I had forgotten the lesson I learned up in Harlem, I'll have you know that I would *not* have Granpapa and Mulgar putting on cork in my house. If they wanted to perform in blackface, they could damn well go out on the front lawn and do it for all I cared, which they sometimes did, much to the delight of the passing motorists.

I believe Mulgar was especially excited to celebrate Christmas with us. Everyone chipped in and bought him an adorable new wardrobe to replace his shabby old clothes. He looked especially smart in his little newsboy outfit with the suspenders and bully boy cap, and after trying it on, he paraded around the room like a right little emperor.

"You're really going to be a hit with the ladies in your new outfits, Mulgar," I teased him. Mulgar beamed with pride.

Daddy and Granpapa bought each other meat baskets, stuffed to the gills with salty jerkeys and meat snackers. They gave me the loveliest little diamond pendant with my name engraved on the back. As rough as things got over the years, I always held onto that pendant as a reminder of the good old days. Myrna asked me to try it on once, and oh daddy, you wouldn't believe the earful she got that day. She can't wear her own jewelry because it turns her neck green. That's what you get for buying that trash from the Home Shopping Club, I tell her, but she doesn't listen to me.

Production for *The Slippery Girls of Grizzly Gulch* began on December 30 1938. Werner Von Growler had directed only one other film for MGM, a B Western called *The Executionist*. Werner had recently fled Nazi Germany, where he had gained a reputation as an artist for filming people sneezing. Adolph Hitler was apparently disgusted by sneezes, and Werner would have been killed for his art if he hadn't emigrated. Werner once held a mandatory screening on set for his masterpiece, *1,000 Sneezes,* and after sitting through that four-hour piece of garbage, I was prepared to kill him then myself. Still, he was a nice man, if a bit odd.

The star of the picture was a lovely and talented actress ten years my senior named Cassie Dixon. I was prepared to hate Cassie's guts, she being the lead in my film, but she actually turned out to be one hell of a gal and a good friend to me over the years. Our relationship got off to a rocky start. At the first read-through, I accidentally threw a cup of coffee in her face. Of course, I waited until the coffee had cooled before I threw it at her. I'm not a monster; I just wanted to give her a little scare. She handled it most graciously, and before I knew it, we were laughing it up like old gal pals.

The day of the read-through, we went around the table and everyone introduced themselves. Cassie played Cat Slippery, the sister of my character, Madge. Playing Cat's love interest would be Royston Krauss, a recent émigré from the British Isles. The young banker who catches Madge's fancy was to be played by the dashingly handsome Archie Chifton. Archie's was the only face in the cast I recognized. He made quite an impression on me a few months earlier when I saw him in the film *Hop 'til You Drop,* an enjoyable little attempt to cash-in on the Lindy Hop craze. My trouble with Tony made me wary to embark upon another relationship, but I fully intended to keep an eye on Archie Chifton, nonetheless.

After the introductions, Werner went over the shooting schedule. My first film was to be a rushed affair with only 25 days of filming scheduled. The entire film was to be shot on soundstages, which seemed to me an odd choice for a film set in a fertile mountain valley that was being shot in a studio surrounded by fertile mountain valleys. One would think that a film taking place in a mountain valley would have at least one shot of a mountain or a valley, but I was not the director, and no one asked me.

Werner then introduced a few members of the crew and outlined the rules of the production. He had a number of strange requests. For starters, we were not allowed to eat in front of him, and if he came into the commissary while we were eating, we were to stop. He said he would not have his actors sitting around with their mouths gaping open like a bunch of filthy cows.

He didn't like flowers, he would not tolerate anyone wearing green, and if we were to catch his eye while we were filming, he insisted that we wash our hands immediately. Other than that, he was one of the more pleasant and easy-going directors I've ever worked with.

The film focused on the trials and tribulations of the Slippery sisters. As the film begins, tomboy Madge and sweet-natured Cat Slippery are tending to their father, an ailing old prospector named Gus (Dashiell Hamilton). Gus we learn, has contracted gulch syndrome from spending his days sifting for gold, and now it is up to the girls to carry on their father's work. Cat leaves her father's bedside to take a walk in the mountains, where she runs into lumberjack Ben Broadly (Krauss). They bicker comically, then sing a song together ("Welcome to My

Mountains, Welcome to My Valley") and fall in love.

The side-plot involved a greedy banker named Mortimer LaRue who was waiting for Gus to die so that he might repossess the land that Gus has worked so hard to keep. The banker sends his protégé, Billy Prawns (Archie) out to our land. Prawns and Madge bicker then fall in love. The film ends happily, with the two sisters winning back their land and having a glorious double-wedding in the mountain. The two couples say their vows and finish with the big finale, "Our Love Is a Golden Nugget." Roll credits.

Although the film was not the worst piece of shit I've ever read, it certainly was not good. Werner wrote the script himself, and his difficulty with the English language was most apparent. The synopsis I just gave you had to be carefully pieced together from a mess of excess dream sequences, side-plots, and unnecessary characters. One four-page scene set in LaRue's office consisted entirely of LaRue and Prawns taking turns sneezing.

I remember where I left my hat pin, or rather, I don't remember ... remember ... I'm sorry, what was I talking about? One moment, please.

Myrna, for the love of God, would you turn off that god ... damned ... redneck music?!? Well, I don't care if it's Willie Nelson or Nelson Eddy, it sounds terrible! I can't even think with that nonsense going on behind me.

Now, where was I? Oh yes, the read-through for *The Slippery Girls*. Yes, well, after the reading, I shared nervous glances with Cassie and Royston and smoldering glances with Archie. "What have we gotten ourselves into?" my eyes said to Cassie and Royston. "I wanna hump you," my eyes said to Archie.

Before the read-through adjourned, Werner led the entire cast and crew through the "Von Growler Pledge," which went, as follows:

I pledge to perform my best for Von Growler
and give my all for Von Growler
and never look at Von Growler
or I will have to wash my hands.

Of course, everything in life looks far more awful in retrospect. At the time, I was terribly happy to be acting in a film, even if it was a potential dud. I didn't care about any stupid old Von Growler Pledge; this was my chance to shine and I wasn't going to let any Nazi ninny boss me around.

When I returned home, Mulgar was all gussied up in an apron and chef's hat. He and Granpapa were making an elderberry pie to celebrate my first day on the set. When I walked in, they both attacked me with sticky hands and kisses on the cheek. I joined them in the kitchen to chat about the film while they baked.

"It seems to me," Granpapa said, after hearing about my day, "that this Von Growler is a little bit of a nutcase."

"Yes," I agreed. "I think he's a lotta bit of a nutcase."

"They all are, kitten, they all are," Granpapa said. "You just pay him no mind. We all know you're a star. Do whatever feels right."

I was happy to have Granpapa back, because he was the only person who would give it to me straight. Everyone else got all worked up in the details, "Oh, Karen, what if Werner doesn't like your performance?" Or, "Karen, shouldn't you listen to other people's opinions?" Granpapa didn't give a flying fig about anyone except for me, Daddy, and Mulgar, and in that respect, we were on exactly the same wavelength. The only opinions that mattered worth a damn were my own and Granpapa's, which were exactly the same as mine.

Werner showed up to our first rehearsal the next day wearing a bee-keeper's outfit. We ran through the script a few times, with Werner giving us tips on how he would like the scenes acted. I found that if I ignored his advice two times in a row, he would not put up a fuss. This was a welcome sign. I was afraid I might have a little bit of a struggle on my hands. But as I came to learn when filming began, Werner did not give a lick about the script, characters, or actors. While we were busy reciting lines and trying to understand his "vision," he was thinking about camera angles and sneezes.

The first scene of the film was shot the very next day. Coming from a theater background, I was astounded by the lack of preparation taken before filming began. According to the other actors, this casual attitude toward quality was not unique to Werner. Only the films with the largest budgets had the luxury of rehearsing their actors.

"Virst zene!" Werner shouted. "I need Madge, Prawns, Broadly, Cat, Gus! Virst zene!"

I took my place and looked over at Werner, who was dressed in a little sailor boy outfit and holding an enormous lollipop.

"Madge! Go vash your hands!" he screamed.

When I returned from the washroom, the cast was assembled on the set, running through their lines.

"Madge! Return! Now ve shoot!"

I found my spot on the set, taking care to avoid looking at Werner.

"Cassie," I whispered, "what scene are we shooting?"

"Prawns's arrival," she said.

The camera operator slapped the clapboard together, Werner raised his megaphone to his mouth, yelled, "Action!" and suddenly, there I was, acting in a Hollywood film.

Excerpt from *The Slippery Girls of Grizzly Gulch*
by W. Von Growler

FADE IN

(Broadly, Madge, and Cat gather near Gus in bed.)

Gus: What is man? Is he the fortune that one tries to find in the rock? Or is he the home one builds with one's sweat and toil? Is he his daughter, or his daughter's lover? What is man?

Madge: I have so much fear!

Cat: Fear is celebration.

Madge: I have so much fear inside!

Broadly and Gus: Fear is SUFFERING.

(A knock comes on the door.)

Prawns: I have orders!

(Broadly opens door.)

Broadly: Who are you?

Prawns: I am Prawns! I have orders!

(Madge begins crying.)

Madge: I have so much fear inside!

Gus (grasping out to uncaring God): It is like a sickness deep inside, her fear!

Prawns: I am smitten! You have smited me! Who is this lovely girl?

Broadly: You'll not know!

(Broadly beats Prawns unmercifully, but necessary. Madge and Cat dodge oranges.)

At this point in the scene, Von Growler began pitching oranges at me and Cassie.

"Avoid zem!" Von Growler screamed. "Avoid ze oranges!"

"The fear comes at me like a knife in the clothing of a lamb!" I wailed. I caught a flash of orange at the edge of my vision and ducked just in time to avoid a direct collision. The orange sailed past me and smacked Dashiell (Gus) directly in the face.

"Ow!" Dashiell said, raising his hands to his face.

"Don't stop acting!" Von Growler screamed. "Avoid ze oranges, you vools!"

"How the fuck am I supposed to avoid the oranges?" Dashiell asked. "I'm trapped in this bed!"

"Gus! Vash your hands!" Von Growler shouted through the megaphone. "Everyone elze continue!"

"How can we continue without Gus?" Prawns asked.

"Prawns! Vash your hands!"

Cassie, Royston and I continued to act the rest of the scene, skipping awkwardly over Dashiell and Archie's lines and ducking from side to side to avoid the onslaught of oranges. At the end of the scene, Werner yelled, "Cut! Print! Wrap!"

The cameras stopped whirring. Cast and crew stared at Werner in astonishment. He removed his sailor hat and placed it on the chair next to him.

"You all do very vell vor virst day," he said. "Now ve shoot ze zong mit Broadly and Cat. You know zis song?"

"I haven't heard it yet," Cassie said.

"Me neither," Royston answered.

"Ha ha ha!" Von Growler laughed jovially. "Ov course you did not hear zis. You did not yet zing it! Ha ha ha."

Von Growler smiled at us all.

"Now, I know vat you tink. You tink mebee my mesids is zomewhat unorsidox. You are right! Von Growler does not do zings like Hollywood! Von Growler does zings like zey do zem in ze vuture!"

He looked around at the thoroughly confused cast and crew, his face beaming with pride.

"Now ve prepare!" he suddenly shouted, and everyone got down to work.

While Werner oversaw the camera and light setups, Cassie and Royston ran through the number frantically a few times with the choreographer and music director. Archie and I sat to the side and watched them rehearse. Or, rather, Archie watched them rehearse, and I watched Archie.

"This is very strange," Archie said. "Shouldn't we know the songs before we attempt to sing them?"

"I agree," I agreed. "It is very strange. We should French kiss."

Archie gave me a funny look.

"What in the world is that?" he asked.

I grabbed his shirt and pulled him into me. He gave me a slightly cold, close-lipped kiss. My tongue shot out of my mouth and pried his lips open, only to bump up against his wall of teeth. Archie pulled back and looked at me in horror.

"My God, Karen, what are you doing?" he asked.

"I'm just giving you a French kiss," I said. "Don't you like it?"

"About as much as a hamburger made of human face!" he squealed. "Ugh, you're disgusting."

"Fine," I said, crossing my arms and slumping back into my seat.

We watched silently from the sidelines as Royston and Cassie were summoned over to the gulch set by a highly excited Werner.

"Let's shoot! Now, now, now!" he shouted.

The cameras rolled, and Cassie and Royston ran through the song and dance routine that they had learned only minutes before. The crew stifled laughs as the two leads stumbled through a painfully embarrassing, half-remembered routine. Werner watched the whole number with an intense look of concentration on his face. When the actors had sung their final notes, Werner shouted, "Now, sneeze!"

"Pardon me?" asked Royston.

"Sneeze! Sneeze you vools! End mit big sneeze! Keep cameras rolling, zing final note, zen sneeze! Go!"

Royston and Cassie hit the final note again, ending in a giant sneeze finale.

"Wunderbar!" Werner shouted. "Now ve are done! Go home you vools!"

"But …" Cassie began to protest.

"Zere is no 'but,' Cat," Werner said, as he placed his sailor hat back on his head and took a lick of his lollipop. "You vere vantastic. Tomorrow ve shoot tree more zenes. Now you rest."

"But we didn't even hit our marks," Royston jumped in.

"Mark, mark, zere iz no mark in life," Werner answered. "You zee, I make it einfach wunderbar."

There was nothing more to be said. Werner left the set, and Cassie, Royston, Archie, and I retired to the commissary for lunch.

"I've worked with some kooks in my time, but this guy takes the cake," Cassie said, as we settled into our seats.

"Rubbish. This director is absolute rubbish," Royston agreed.

"This film is going to be an unmitigated disaster," offered Archie

"Well, it will if you have that kind of attitude," I said.

The three older actors scowled at me, as people are wont to do when you puncture an optimistic hole in their clouds of negativity.

"Don't you see?" I asked them. "Werner Von Growler doesn't give a lick about the acting part of the movie. That means we have to give a lick about it. We can make this movie as good or as bad as we choose. Now, if this is any indication of how the shoot is going to go, I say we wait until Werner has left the set every day, and we spend the afternoons rehearsing for the next day's shoot."

The actors chewed their lunches thoughtfully and thought thoughtfully about my words.

"All right," Royston said.

The other two agreed. And so began Project Undermine the Film by Rehearsing After-Hours and Actually Making It Good.

Agreed, the name was a bit awkward, but remember, this was in the days before every conversation could be boiled down into a "talking point." We had the attention span to say a name like that back then. Ask an actress nowadays to join you in a plan called "Project Undermine the Film by Rehearsing After Hours and Actually Making it Good" and she'll be in the bathroom vomiting up her lunch before you can get the third word out.

Chapter Eighteen
A Starlet Is Born

And so the project got underway. Every morning, we would shoot Werner's vision, and every evening, the four leads would get together and direct the next day's activities. My fellow cast members turned out to be quite a talented bunch, and between working on songs and dialogue, we got to be quite close with one another.

Cassie Dixon, as I mentioned, was an all-around upstanding woman, and a fine hoofer. She was no Alice Faye in the vocal department, but she had a really lovely timbre to her vibrato when she was able to hit the correct notes.

Royston Krauss came from a theater background. He made his reputation in England as Detective Toland Mulgrew in the popular IBC radio program *The Esther Prim Mysteries*. Royston is the only actor I've ever known who could communicate his entire range of theatrical emotions strictly with his voice. Where the rest of the cast relied heavily on facial and body movements to convey the emotion of the lines, Royston tended to stand stock still, delivering his lines through a soft, barely-moving face. It was really an extraordinary thing to witness for those of us who are used to seeing films acted by humans who behave as humans do.

Archie Chifton was a mediocre actor, an unbearable human being, a tone-deaf singer, and an absolutely irresistible man. He had wavy red hair slicked back Chicago style and the facial features of a young Fred Astaire. At 5'4", he was a few inches shorter than me. To compensate for this emasculating difference in height on the set, Werner made Archie stand on a pile of books in all of our scenes. For the dance scenes, Werner would set up multiple piles of books, and Archie would jump from pile to pile as I furiously tried to keep up with him.

As so often happens on movie sets, romance blossomed between the two respective couples. Royston and Cassie took to each other immediately. Mere days after filming began, the two were walking around as though they had been born holding onto one another's genitals. By contrast, Archie and I got off to a rather rocky start. One day he would proclaim his utter devotion to me, and the next he would disavow my existence. It was maddening and intoxicating all at once, and sometimes one at a time.

At a mere 23 years old, Archie was the youngest man I had ever pursued. He was still seven years my senior, of course. I was hardly robbing any cradles. I found it grandly ironic when I first told Daddy about my infatuation. "Doesn't he seem awfully old for you?" Daddy asked.

"Not really," I said. "I usually date men who are in their forties."

"Ha, ha," he said. "You're joking, right?"

"Of course, Daddy," I replied, giving him a kiss on the cheek.

Filming progressed with daily doses of odd behavior from Werner. The day Archie and I shot our first love scene, Werner arrived on a pony.

"Today," he exclaimed, "ze pony shall be Von Growler! Now rezite ze Pony Pledge!"

In unison, we chanted:

I pledge to perform my best for the pony
and give my all for the pony
and never look at the pony
or I will have to wash my hands.

It is extremely difficult, I learned, to avert your eyes from a pony that is wearing a beret and riding crops. I must have washed my hands five times during that scene, nearly missing Cat's final bit of dialogue with Prawns. Luckily, we had rehearsed the scene to death the evening before, and I was able to skate in just as the cameras started rolling and give a flawless performance worthy of several major awards which, sadly, I have yet to receive.

Another time, during the filming of the final scene at the gulch, Werner suspended himself from the rafters with a rope and flew around the stage, sprinkling sand on our heads as we emoted. The actors squinted and blinked at one another as the sand flew dangerously close to our eyes. All except for Royston, who lacked the ability to blink.

The final day of filming, Werner gathered us together for one last go-round of the Von Growler Pledge.

"Bevore ve zay ze pledge today," he began, I vould like to zank you all vor your pazience during zis trying film zhoot. I know I am not ze easy man to vork vor, but you do nize zings, and you zhall zee in ze vilm zat ze vision is genius. Today, during ze vilmink, you may look at Von Growler. But only vor a zplit zecond, and zen you must act!"

He smiled benevolently at the cast and crew as we clapped politely. We were no dumb chickens; we knew the film was going to be a mess. But everyone was getting paid, and despite Von Growler's eccentricities, he meant well. At various times during the shoot he had pulled each of the actors aside and roused our spirits in the way that only descendants of the Germanic tribes can. Not even the most hardened crew-member on the set could withstand his efficient, economical charms. He was always happy with our performances, regardless of how well we actually performed, and the only time I saw him lose his temper was the day that the D.P. showed up wearing a green suit with a flower pinned to his lapel. Which, really, you can't blame Werner for that one. He made it quite clear to everyone that he hated green and flowers.

At the wrap party, I shared my first reciprocated off-screen kiss with Archie. Yes, I was moving quite slow for me. No, it was not by choice. His reaction to the initial French kiss had quite offended me, and I made a pledge to myself that I would not give him the opportunity again until I felt he was good and ready. But then I got sick of waiting, so I pulled him out of the buffet line and stuck my tongue down his throat.

This time, he was far more receptive to my advances, and we spent the night dancing and frenching under the light of a pale Los Angeles moon.

It was an absolutely marvelous night to be young and alive. Cassie, Royston, Archie, and I got rip-roaring drunk on Mexican wine and led the cast and crew through sing-along after sing-along. Werner, who arrived wearing a potato sack and a lady's wig, got so smashed that he tried to start a fight with an ice sculpture.

After the party, the four of us went back to Royston's house to continue our celebrations. Now, it is a hard and fast rule that, if a group of actors get together, talk will turn to sex within fifteen minutes. I have my theories as to why this rule exists. For one, since the dawn of the silent era, actors and actresses have fancied themselves a progressive community. For two, we do not have much else to talk about. And for three, we are all unbelievably attractive and our libidos have been scientifically proven to operate at ten times the speed of regular human beings.

Royston, the old hound dog, was the one who got the ball rolling, with a suggestion that Cassie and I remove our shirts and kiss. We complied with the kiss, but we insisted that he and Archie reveal their peckers before we remove our shirts. It was not long before we were all naked in the living room of Royston's bungalow, kissing and touching one another's lips and private parts.

As anyone who has been involved in an impromptu orgy might tell you, it all happened rather quickly, and with little acknowledgment as to what we were doing. One bit of advice I can give for anyone hoping to experience "the love that has many backs:" once genitalia has been exposed, there is no turning back. If you show your genitals at enough social functions, someone will eventually take you up on the deal, and the dominoes will fall quickly from thence forward. For are we not all sexual creatures, a few laws away from ripping each other's clothing off and copulating in the streets? We humans fancy ourselves so refined, with our penises and vaginas hidden away behind sheets of fabric. But just go ahead and get it out there; you'll see what happens.

I don't claim that it is a good thing to be perpetually striving for sexual gratification, mind you. We are conflicted, you see, by our desire to be in a constant state of orgasmic bliss and our mind's inclination to form little protective communities with other people. Swapping off partners in a protective community can have a volatile outcome, unless each member of said community has a sociopathic inability to form attachments with others. Although I did not mind watching Archie take Cassie from behind while Royston tickled my forehead with his testicles, had this been our continual state of affairs, what started as an erotic adventure may have eventually become a catalyst for jealousy.

But as a one-night experience, it was most enjoyable. Archie turned out to be a passionate lover, though it took quite some time and cajoling by Royston for him to get aroused. His eyes remained fixated on Royston throughout the ordeal, watching the more experienced actor for guidance and support. I tried to turn his focus toward me several times to no avail. Archie was nothing if not eager to learn from the wisdom of others. When we were shooting the film, seldom did Royston shoot a scene without Archie sitting off to the side of the stage, immersed in the older actor's performance.

It took me some days after the wrap party to recover from the intense experience I had just been through. I had not been able to spend much time with my family during the month of filming, as every second that was not devoted to rehearsals or shoots was spent drinking with my fellow cast members. Mulgar, in particular, was overjoyed to have me back home. I walked in the door the morning after the wrap party to find him passed out on the couch beneath a banner reading "Congratulations, Karen." The poor dear had been up nearly the entire night, waiting for me to return. I roused him with a light kiss on the forehead, and we sat in the kitchen together, sipping coffee in blissful silence.

I gave a large part of the paycheck for my first film to Daddy, who used it to pay off Granpapa's medical bills and a large portion of our house. The Great Depression had left many of my generation wary of banks, and the 10,000 or so dollars that remained after my generous gift went straight into a suitcase that I kept in the back of my closet. In those days, $10,000 was a king's ransom. I felt absolutely on top of the world.

I spent the next few months on vacation, attending Hollywood parties and eagerly checking the trades for mentions of my name. A few film offers came in through Pauly Auskie, but Granpapa and I agreed my best move was to hold out for an A-list picture. At the time, my stance was considered somewhat unusual by those in the industry. Back then, unknown actors were expected to thrust themselves at any opportunity that crossed their paths. Well, not me, brother. I was not about to waste my talent in some two-bit wrestling picture, not when I was convinced that the upper echelons of film society would soon be waiting in line to knock on my door.

Archie was of a different mindset, and a mere three days after our erotic encounter, he was off to Northern California to shoot a war picture entitled *The Boys of Company B*. Although it was a painful experience at the time, it turned out to be the best thing that could have happened to our relationship. Through our phone calls and letters, I learned a lot more about Archie than I probably would have if we had been engaged in a face-to-face relationship. He was a lovely writer, and I have turned back to those letters time and again throughout my life when I need to be reminded of those innocent, carefree days.

The premiere for *Slippery Girls* was held on April 20 1940, just five days after my eighteenth birthday. Mulgar had taught himself to design clothing and sew while staying at my house, and he whipped me up a lovely taffeta number that could have easily been on display in the showrooms of the most luxurious Hollywood designers.

Mulgar, Daddy, and Granpapa were my dates for the evening. They all got gussied up in tuxedoes, and, boy, you would have thought they were a bunch of women the way they fretted. Cummerbunds, cuff links, and hair finally in place, the four of us climbed into the studio's limo and off we drove on a one-way trip to a place called "fame."

My heart raced as I alit from the limo and stared down the red carpet at the theater entrance. Of course, when *The Slippery Girls* debuted, America did not have the same sort of entertainment press that we have nowadays. There were no twenty-four hour television channels or nightly gossip programs devoted to sucking the life out of every last detail of the creative process. So the experience of walking the red carpet was, at least in the case of a smaller picture like *The Slippery Girls,* not the screaming, bodyguard-intensive affair that one might imagine. Today, the studios can conjure up fistfuls of baboons to stand around screaming at their premieres, no matter how little the film is anticipated or how few celebrities are featured in it. The theory being, of course, that people watching at home will see the footage on their *ETVs* or their *Entertainment Tonights* and turn to one another and say, "Look at all that excitement! Those people are so very excited to see that movie! That must mean the movie is exciting!" And then they will go and spend their hard-earned money to see what all the screaming excitement is about. In reality, most people would much rather watch the coverage of the premiere than the movie being covered. It is more entertaining to watch people standing outside of a theater screaming than to be inside the theater watching the terrible film that those people are screaming about.

No one was screaming outside of our theater, but the press was out in full force. I was very excited, until I started to look at the names on the microphones and cameras and press passes and realized that I did not recognize a single one of them. The reporters lining the red carpet wore long, heavy trench coats and mumbled quietly into their microphones in German. "Hitler," I heard more than one of them say, as we passed. I looked at Granpapa. He seemed oblivious to the odd behavior of the reporters, and he waved happily for the cameras as we walked into the theater.

Once inside, we took our seats next to the other leads and their families. Archie was still away shooting *The Bugle Boys of Company B,* but Cassie and Royston and the rest of the cast greeted me and my family warmly. Werner said a few brief words about the film, the lights dimmed, and the movie began.

Much to everyone's surprise and delight, *The Slippery Girls of Grizzly Gulch* turned out to be not half bad. It was not even one quarter bad. It was quite good, actually. The skilled editing of longtime Von Growler collaborator J.P. Mindlehoff turned what may have very well been a disaster on the scale of the *Titanic* into a highly enjoyable romantic picture like Titanic. Our secret rehearsals filled in the blanks for what turned out to be some rather innovative directorial decisions on the part of Von Growler. During the scene where he pelted us with oranges, for instance, the terror at getting hit by the flying orbs translated into concern for the well-being of our father and, on Gus's part, a fear of dying before he could give his daughters the life he had always promised. Mindlehoff skillfully cut around the oranges, so that the audience saw only the reactions on our faces.

Sadly, our little film never stood a chance in the backwards studio system of the 1930s. *The Slippery Girls* was a B-picture, which meant that it ran as the second film of a double-bill. No one ordered B-pictures, they were handed to the exhibitors as incentives for taking the A-pictures. We had the misfortune of being paired with a really awful tear-jerker called *A Broken Bough,* which was gone from the theaters in a matter of weeks. Still, it was magical to finally see myself on the silver screen, and I will maintain to my grave that *The Slippery Girls* is an overlooked American classic. Or at the very least, it is an enjoyable way to waste an hour and twenty minutes of what I presume to be your miserable lives.

Von Growler went on to direct a few more Hollywood pictures, most notably *The Dark Side of a Whistle,* the only American film starring Romanian screen-idol Ivor LeFrench. After the war, Werner returned back home to Germany, where I am told he opened a sneezing museum.

An interesting side note: I learned years later that the film actually generated quite a bit of controversy back in Germany. The Nazi paparazzi that stood outside on the red carpet during the premiere mistakenly identified me as a relative of der fuehrer himself, and Adolph took a small bit of heat from his underlings when they learned that his distant cousin appeared in a film directed by one of their most despised expatriates. I hear the rumors upset Hitler greatly, and I like to think that I played a large role in his eventual suicide. I don't care what your Holocaust revisionist friends might tell you; that man was not to be trusted.

Chapter Nineteen
To Love, Perchance to Dream

Archie returned to Los Angeles a few days after the premiere. Our love had blossomed while he was away, and we often spent late hours on the telephone, making love and discussing future plans together. As I got to know him better, I learned that his initial hesitations with me were the result of a deep-rooted distrust of relationships that stemmed from being brought up by a clinically insane mother and an emotionally distant father. The horror stories he told me about his childhood made my upbringing seem positively enchanted by comparison. His mother spent most of her days crying in her bedroom while his father paraded around town with women of the night. Young Archie and his beloved sister Clarabelle were sometimes dragged along on his father's dates, where they were often introduced by their father as "some kids I know."

At age 16, Archie left home and moved in with his eccentric great-uncle in Los Angeles. Archie took a job as a short-order cook. He was forging a decent living, content with the blue-collar life, when a casting agent discovered him at one of his uncle's pool parties. The untrained Archie turned out to be quite a capable actor, and when I met him, he had already appeared in seven films.

Archie's youth and vulnerability were a nice change from the hardened, crusty old pricks for whom I usually fell. For the first time, I felt as though my lover needed me as much as I needed him ... not more so, like Fletcher, or less so, like Tony. I immediately set to incorporating him into my family life.

Unfortunately, my family was not quite as interested in incorporating Archie. My father, in particular, took an immediate dislike to my new boyfriend. Shortly after Archie returned from filming, I invited him over to dinner. Archie, it should be noted, was quite proud of his Irish ancestry. A side course of potatoes led to a political discussion about the Irish famine, which erupted into a bitter argument. Much as I loved my father, he could be a stubborn man when it came to potatoes.

But Daddy loved me, and he was determined to let me live my life in the way that I saw fit. Granpapa had little concern one way or the other. "If you're happy, Karen," he said, "then I'm happy. Even if your boyfriend is a poofter."

That was another thing that bothered Daddy; Archie was what we would refer to today as "flamboyantly gay." It would take many years for me to discover this, of course, and several more to admit it. Daddy and Granpapa knew right away. I had yet to be exposed to the homosexual subculture of Los Angeles, and Archie seemed to me like the best of all possible worlds: the sensitivity of a woman with the penis of a man.

On the career front, Pauly Auskie was hard at work getting me auditions for other films. I auditioned for a number of pictures at the end of '39, and I finally landed a small role in a first run melodrama called *The Limpers.* I played Cecile Cardiff, a nurse who worked in the polio ward where the majority of the film took place. It was a small role, but I made the most of it, as was my gift. *Variety* noted in their review that I was "a visible presence."

New Year's Eve, 1939, came filled with promise, hope, and excitement for the coming decade. Archie and I celebrated at the home of his eccentric Uncle Peter. Uncle Peter had made his fortune as the owner of a chain of furriers that catered to upper-class Asian women. Their ads were ubiquitous on Los Angeles radio: "Uncle Peter's puts the slink in the mink and the Chink in the chinchilla."

If Archie seemed flamboyant, his uncle was positively vaginal. That New Year's Eve, I was the only woman at a party filled with the half-naked young studs who Uncle Peter referred to as his "man harem." Although Archie had told me about his uncle's sexual proclivities, I will admit, I was unprepared to spend an evening watching men beating one another off with rubber tourniquets. It would be many years before the concept of homosexuality as a genetic trait became accepted, and the guests at Uncle Peter's party seemed decadent at best, terrifying at worst.

Uncle Peter had a longtime companion known as Mister Mary who gave me the willies, and not in an erotic way. Before the party even started, he was soused beyond all recognition, and his repeated offers to "tickle Archie's pickle for a nickel" grew less and less charming as the night progressed. Finally, at the end of the night, I simply would not stand for it anymore.

"Leave him alone!" I shouted at Mister Mary. "You may delight in rubbing your genitals against other men, but my Archie will not be drawn into your perverse activities!"

"Not with you here, Dearie," Mister Mary drawled, a wicked sparkle in his eye, "but if you think lover-boy impressed that casting agent with his acting talents, you've got another think coming."

As much as I liked to fancy myself a lady, I would not stand for some dried-up old queen making untoward allegations about my lover. I attacked him with the viciousness of a pit bull, screaming and clawing at his face until Archie pulled me off. Mister Mary backed away, tears and mascara running down his sunken cheeks. "You brute!" he shouted. "You damnable Baltimore brute!" With the party-goers screaming bloody murder behind us, Archie grabbed me by the hand, and off we fled in his automobile.

We celebrated the turn of the decade by making love in the parking lot of Mr. Friendlier's. Afterwards, Archie held me in his arms and stroked my hair tenderly.

"Do you love me, Karen?" he asked.

"Yes," I replied, filled to bursting with dreams and semen.

"Would you like to be my wife?" he asked.

In the heat of the moment and the headlights of the passing drunkards, Archie seemed to me a protective and nurturing god, fallen to Earth to lead me through a lifetime of marital bliss. I did not think twice before accepting. I probably should have. But I was young and in love with an effeminate boy and the stars that reflected in his pomade.

We broke the news to my family the next day. Although my father was well-skeptical, he recognized that my love for Archie was true and strong, and he reluctantly gave his blessing. Granpapa was overjoyed at my happiness, and he popped open a very special bottle of champagne that he had been saving for just such an important occasion.

As we drank our toast, I noticed that one member of the family was missing. I excused myself from the proceedings and walked out to the veranda, where Mulgar sat sullenly on a bench, pitching rocks at the fence that lined our small property.

"Hello, Mulgar," I said.

Mulgar stared sadly into the distance, ignoring my presence.

"Mulgar, what's wrong?" I asked, concerned.

He said nothing.

"Is this about the wedding?" I whispered, leaning in close to him.

Slowly, Mulgar nodded his head.

"You don't think I should marry Archie, do you?" I asked.

Mulgar shook his head, "non."

"Is it because you think he's secretly a homosexual and the only reason I'm marrying him is because I'm an incredibly needy person who reacts on the spur of the moment instead of thinking things through properly?"

Mulgar looked at me with a puzzled expression on his face and shook his head.

"Then what is it, Mulgar? What reason could you possibly have for objecting to this marriage?"

Tears welled in Mulgar's eyes as he stared into mine. I wasn't going to budge. This time, I would not be filling in Mulgar's sentiments with my own words. If he had a problem with my pending nuptials, he could damn well tell me himself.

Finally, after what seemed like an eternity, Mulgar spoke.

"Hi ..." he began, then paused.

"Hello," I answered, on the edge of my seat. It was the first word I had heard him speak in months.

"Hi ..." he began again.

"Say it, Mulgar," I pleaded, tears beginning to form in my eyes.

"Your opinion means the world to me. If you don't approve of this marriage, then I don't know what."

Mulgar pushed all of his strength into his tiny brown face. Lips quivering, he finally finished his thought.

"Hi loth you."

I reeled back against the bench. His words struck me like a mallet strikes a gong, his words being the mallet and my face being the gong. Could it be true? Could little Mulgar, my best friend and closest confidante, could he have been nursing a secret love for me over the last year? It made perfect sense; after all, I was probably one of the few people who had shown him kindness in his wretched little life, and I was really quite beautiful. If I were Mulgar, I would probably be stroking my little wang to visions of myself, as well.

In what stood as foreshadowing for the future of our relationship, Archie came out at a very inopportune time. The hatred on Mulgar's face was palatable as Archie stood behind me and cradled my head in his hands.

"Hello, Mulgar," he said. "How are ya', buddy? Ya' getting excited for the wedding?"

Mulgar pitched a rock against the fence, where it hit with a hollow thud.

"Your father and I were just having the most marvelous conversation about Irish linen," Archie said to me. "I believe this marriage might work itself out, after all. Come back inside, dear. We're thinking of grilling flank steaks."

I looked at Mulgar, whose lips were pursed in a mixture of anger and sadness. In a decision that I would regret for quite some time, I rose from the bench and returned with Archie to the living room.

Our wedding took place in March under a lilac tree in the backyard of Uncle Peter's mansion. Due to the shooting schedules of our respective films, (he was playing the male lead in RKO's *The Big Stretch* and I was co-starring in Republic's *Macintosh Butterfly*), we had to hold the wedding on a Wednesday. I was somewhat hesitant to hold the ceremony on Uncle Peter's property, what with my negative experience on New Year's, but Archie convinced me that Mister Mary was going to attend no matter where we held the ceremony, and better to take the fight to the enemy than hold the wedding in some distasteful V.F.W. hall.

I wish I could tell you the details of that glorious day, but the truth is, I was drunk from the minute I awoke on the morning of the wedding 'til the time we returned from our honeymoon. Mulgar's disapproval really hit me hard, and for the first time in my life, I started consciously drinking to forget. To his credit, Mulgar managed to rally himself to attend the wedding. I vaguely remember having a heartfelt conversation with him at the reception. It was assuredly one of the "20 Questions" style conversations I was used to with Mulgar, because he would not speak another word for several years following his confession of love.

We honeymooned in Niagara Falls as was the style at the time. I can't tell you a thing about the city. I vaguely remember it being Canadian and filled with giant water fountains or something. Archie spent the honeymoon drunk, as well, most likely trying to cover up his latent homosexuality.

I returned to shoot a few final scenes of *Macintosh Butterfly*. I was playing another supporting role, this time as the best friend of a female detective. My role was rather inconsequential in the plot of the film, but I had a few solid moments. I don't recall a lot about that shoot. I have since read that the film was directed by Hiller Benjamin, who of course went on to great success as the creator of the *Mrs. Policat* shorts. I couldn't pick the man out of a police line-up, although I have a vague memory of vomiting on his shoes at the release party.

I should probably apologize at this point for my rather sketchy remembrances of this period of my life. I'm trying to fill in the gaps as best I can, but the truth is, I was drinking so much during this time that my memory is somewhat lacking. Certain moments stand out, such as the time I threatened to walk off the set of *Come, You Pilgrims* if I didn't get a ham sandwich right that very moment, a ham sandwich which never arrived, because no one really cared if I wanted a ham sandwich or not, because I was a stock actress who could be replaced in a heartbeat. That was fun. There was another story I remember... about working on a film that starred a horse... *Myrna, do you remember that one? The one with the horse? Yes, I played a young girl in love with a horse who played cricket. How can you not remember? Oh, come, you must*

*remember the film where I costarred with a horse. Well, I costarred with
the person who costarred with the horse, anyway. You don't remember?
God, woman, I'm going to renounce your position as the honorable
founder of my fan club, if you don't get your head together. Yes, there
are still members. Have you checked the web traffic lately? Well, it's an
interesting phenomenon, if you'd get your head out of your ass and
admit that time didn't stop in fucking 1972!*

I'm sorry, reader. You must realize that I'm transcribing these
notes from a tiny apartment in the Hollywood Friends Adult Condo
development. I am trying to keep the modern world out of our mono-
logue, as I completely recognize that this story might seem somewhat
depressing if you're dealing with my present life before you've fully
digested my past life. But from time to time, the modern world will
creep in, necessarily, seeing as how this is the life in which I live at the
present time. Ugh. This whole biographical process is ridiculous. I can't
believe I ever agreed to it in the first place. And why do I need this
ghostwriter? All this person seems to be doing is transcribing exactly
what I'm saying and putting the commas in the right place. I don't know
why I can't just put the thing on paper myself.

I have no idea what I'm doing. Hear this loud and clear, readers:
autobiographies are nonsense. As though anyone can remember what
someone said to them seventy years ago. Just because I've lived a
more fabulous and fascinating life than you will ever experience does-
n't mean my memory's any better than yours. Can you tell me what you
had for breakfast two days ago? Unless it was some kind of special
breakfast that you cooked up for your sweetheart or the routine breakfast that you eat every day, you cannot. Memory is flawed. Imagine that
you are trying to recall that breakfast you ate sixty-five years in the
future. Not that easy, is it?

I'm sorry, am I breaking the fourth wall? I apologize. I know you
want to believe that everyone's life is neatly laid out in book form, but
it just doesn't work that way. Life is complex. An event that seems sig-
nificant today might seem totally inconsequential forty years in the
future. When you're writing your life story, what becomes important? Is
it the way a hint of perfume tickles your nostril when you're making
love, or is it the twisted position of a dead armadillo baking in the sun

on a lonely Arizona road? If YOU think, for ONE SECOND, that your story means something in the grand pantheon of literature, then YOU are a complete idiot. *And Myrna... for Chrissakes, woman, refill my GOD-DAMNED drink! For CHRISSAKES, I'm half MAD with the way the man down the hall, you know the one, with the goofy teeth...*

(speech unintelligible)

Chapter Twenty

The Years that Will Live in Infamy

Goddamn, did I get drunk last night.

Continuing ... must continue ... where were we? Ah yes. Married life.

I remember it like it was yesterday. December 7 1941. "The day that will live in infamy," or, as it is more popularly known, D-Day. When I heard the news on the radio, I broke down in tears. The United States was officially involved in the Second World War, and I was officially a widow.

1941 had started out innocently enough. After our wedding, I moved into Archie's house at the foot of the Hollywood Hills. We were the perfect picture of marital bliss. My family came to accept Archie as a member of the family-the gay one. He fit in well with our cast of lovable misfits, and even Mulgar eventually accepted the reality that Archie was here to stay. On Saturdays, Mulgar would come over for tea, and we would play Tickle-Tackle and Bobsy-Gators until it was time to go to sleep.

Archie was a dear, dear friend during those early days. Contrary to what might be expected from a gay husband, our love life was actually quite robust. He was my first introduction to role-playing, a convention that opened up whole new realms of sexual possibilities for me. Archie loved swashbuckling pirate scenarios, whereas I rather enjoyed playing

Victorian petticoat dramas. In one of my favorite scenarios, Archie played the prim and proper Lady Pennington, while I was the exotic and mysterious Duke of Kerchief. We would begin with me bursting into his boudoir lasciviously, where he would be freshening his powder.

"I dare say!" he would dare say. "Have you not the proper respect for a lady of affluence, you swine? Can you not see that I am in my under drawers?"

"'Tis but a gateway to your ripened flesh," I would say. "Come, Lady Pennington, let me ravish you on the trundle bed."

Then I would guide him to the bed and we would strip one another down to our wigs and have passionate sex in the bodies and minds of other people. It was most delicious fun. Whoever tells you that straights and gays can't have passionate sexual relationships simply doesn't have enough creativity.

On the career front, after *Come, You Pilgrims* and some horse movie, I played supporting roles in four more films for Republic and two more for RKO, or so my filmography claims. I merited a few mentions in the dailies here and there, most notably for my role in *The Gates of Poseidon*. I played Ichthes, the sea witch who is hypnotized to do Poseidon's bidding. In my major scene, I address an army of mermen who are off to the Peloponnesian War.

> Swim, you fishlike men, you gods of the sea! Advance upon Peloponnesus! Shave the hair from the goat of Andrelychus and bring it to me! From this, I will create a potion that will free us from the confines of the sea. No longer shall the mer-people live in fear of men and boats!

As the last line rang out, a bolt of lightning flew down from the sky and knocked me from my parapet. My death scene was brutal and emotionally draining, and more than one reviewer mentioned my death as the highlight of the film.

My alcoholism continued, unabated. Somehow, I managed to hide my problem from everyone except Archie, who drank as much if not more than I did, and Mulgar, who ... well, who really cared what Mulgar thought. It wasn't like he was going to go blabbing my secret all over town, the little mute.

Part of the problem, I think, was the roles I was getting. I had hoped that I would be able to move up the MGM ladder after *Slippery Girls*, but this was not the case. Instead, I was stuck on the lateral sidewalk of the B-picture actress, never gaining recognition, never moving forward, just plodding along in one stinker after another. I was too smart to accept my fate with a smile, and I could not possibly perform my job without deadening my soul and brain cells before each line reading.

Pauly Auskie, to his credit, did not give up on me. He submitted my picture and resume to every major film in production. I was making fine money doing the B-pictures, but I was spending it rather quickly on booze and turkey memorabilia for my collection. Archie and I lived like a couple of queens on our money, buying expensive clothing for our fancy meals out at the finest restaurants.

We continued to socialize with Cassie and Royston. Although I spent many nights dreaming of another romp in the sack with them, Archie had been rather psychologically damaged by our initial encounter, and he politely told us all that group sex was not his bag. I was so in love with Archie that I repressed my desire for further sexual adventures, a decision I regret to this day. Some psychologists might call this unhealthy; I call it coping.

In the fall of 1941, Archie and I both landed our first starring roles. I won the role of Pidgin Elderstein in Tom Fancy's *The Bountiful Good Earth*, and Archie got the part of Major Devon McCulloch in Alistair Logan's *The Pipes of War*. Royston was also cast in *The Pipes of War*, playing Archie's second-in-command. The film was shot on location in Hawaii. Paramount had received special permission to shoot the naval scenes aboard the U.S.S. Arizona in Pearl Harbor. Cue foreboding music … now.

On November 24 1941, Archie and Royston shipped off to Hawaii for a three-week shooting vacation. Cassie and I were both seething with jealousy at our lovers' luck. Sadly, professional jealousy is par for the course in a relationship between two actors. If I had a nickel for every one of my relationships that was destroyed by casting decisions, I would be a very wealthy woman indeed, or toasted to the gills on an unlimited supply of tequila and crack.

I took some solace in the knowledge that *The Bountiful Good Earth* was a good script that might make for a fine film. Tom Fancy was one of the more bankable B-picture directors, thanks to the unexpected success of his last film, *To Walk with Destiny*, a film I enjoyed very much. He was an utmost professional on the set, only rarely throwing me off the lot for drunk and disorderly behavior.

The afternoon of December 7 1941, I awoke sometime in the afternoon and flipped on the radio. Cassie and I had tied one on the night before at a birthday party for Cassie's dear friend Vivien Oakland, with whom Cassie appeared in *A Chump at Oxford* in 1940. If we were trashed, Viv was nuclear wasted. In the wee small hours of the morning the three of us escaped the party, hopped a fence, and took a dip in the fetid lagoon down the road from her house. It was touch and go for a moment there as Viv nearly choked to death on a frog. Luckily, she managed to swallow the little guy, which made Cassie and I laugh so hard that we vomited all over one another. It was a messy evening, all right, and I was just about ready to pour myself a reviving glass of gin when I heard the shocking news.

"If you're just joining us, you should know that only moments ago, a battalion of Japanese bombers attacked the United States Naval Base in Pearl Harbor, Hawaii. Several ships have been damaged, and we're getting reports that some of the ships have been sunk, including the USS Oklahoma, the USS California, and the USS Arizona."

A gasp arose in my throat at the mention of the Arizona. I ran to the refrigerator and checked the shooting schedule Archie left behind. "December 7 1941," I read. "McCulloch and Foister: fight aboard Arizona. Call time: 7:00 AM."

"Nooooo!" I screamed, clawing at the refrigerator door. "Nooooo!" I tore the magnets from the refrigerator and hurled them at the kitchen window. "Nooooo!" I grabbed a hold of the fruit bowl atop the refrigerator and slumped against the refrigerator door, sliding down, down, down until I hit the ground, bananas and grapes showering upon my head like citric hailstones. I lay on the ground, sobbing among the fruit.

At that moment, Daddy and Mulgar ran in the front door. Spying me on the ground, they each grabbed an arm. "Good lord, Karen!"

Daddy roared. "You smell like a damned New Orleans vomit factory!" I wailed and slashed at the air with my claws as they attempted to raise me into a chair. Daddy pinned me to the chair, as I cried and clawed until he finally managed to calm me down to a gentle sob.

"Mulgar and I were on our way to bocce practice when we heard the news," Daddy said. "Have you tried to contact the studio yet? Does anyone know anything?"

"Noooo!" I wailed. "He's deeead. Deeeeeead!"

"Dammit, Karen, pull yourself together!" Daddy snapped, giving me a firm whack across my cheek. "They may have killed your husband, but those bastards attacked my country!"

Daddy's callousness sent me into new hysterics.

"Goddamn, you smell like trash!" Daddy yelled. "Mulgar, I can hardly stand it!"

Mulgar, ever the dear, knew just what I needed. He quietly and nobly braved the odor and wrapped his arms around me. His caring grasp gave me the comfort I need to calm the fuck down.

Daddy got on the phone and dialed Archie's agent, Rusty Peet. Rusty hadn't heard from Archie or the studio, but he promised he would call as soon as word arrived.

With Daddy and Mulgar on phone patrol, I took a much needed bath. Crying, I scrubbed the swamp and vomit and alcohol from my skin. If I could just get clean, I felt, I could bring my husband back from the dead. Thanks to many years of therapy with the wonderful Dr. Brody, I am now able to recognize that this moment marked the beginning of my obsessive compulsive disorder. OCD was unrecognized at the time that I developed it, of course, and it was often misdiagnosed as "crazy." But I digress.

Daddy and Mulgar stayed into the evening with me, listening to the radio and crying. It had been awhile since we'd had a nice cry together. I often think back fondly upon that evening, sharing a warm cup of tea around the radio and all having a jolly good cry over the death of my husband. It's moments like these that you cherish as an actress, the small moments that make life worth living.

At around 9:00, we received a phone call from the studio, telling us that the entire crew aboard the Arizona had perished.

"The crew of the ship or the crew of the film?" Daddy asked.

"We'll have to get back to you on that," the studio answered.

Midnight rolled around, and still, no word regarding Archie's whereabouts. I knew it was hopeless. Had Archie been alive, he would have called. He would have fought tooth and nail to get to a telephone and call his beloved wife, Navy regulations be damned. I went to bed and fell into a dreamless sleep.

The next morning, I was awakened by a telephone call. I raised the receiver to my ear and heard the news I had long dreaded.

"Mrs. Chifton, this is Arnold Ziffer from Paramount Pictures. We regret to inform you that your husband has been caught fornicating with another man."

"My husband?" I exclaimed. "My husband died, sir, aboard the USS Arizona, and I do not find this gag to be a very humorous one."

"I'll tell you what, why don't I let him explain?"

Archie got on the phone.

"My darling?" Archie said.

"My darling!" I shouted.

"Darling, there's something I must tell you. I was not aboard the USS Arizona when it sank. I was sleeping with Royston."

"Why would you be sleeping with Royston?" I asked, puzzled.

"Well, you see, it's a rather absurd story, darling," Archie began. "It seems that some crazed Hawaiian slipped some sort of drug into our poi the evening before. I awoke to find that, during the course of the evening, someone had stripped us naked and put us in Royston's bed with my penis in his rectum!"

"The brutes!" I cried. "The depraved fiends!"

"Exactly what I said, my darling. Well, you can imagine my horror when the police barged in to tell us that not only had we missed the shoot, the Arizona had been attacked, and we were both headed to jail on some trumped up sodomy charges!"

"It's all a mix-up! A terrible, horrible, no good, very bad mix-up! Tell them, darling," I pleaded. "Tell them you're a married man. Tell them about Lady Pennington and the Duke of Kerchief!"

"I did, my darling, but they simply refused to believe me. I thought for certain that Royston and I would rot away in this damned tropical jail, but thank God, Mr. Ziffer came and bailed us out."

"He's a good man, Mr. Ziffer," I averred. "A fine American."

"Indeed, darling," Archie agreed. "However, I must warn you, there were photographers waiting at the station. I'm terribly afraid my career may be ruined."

"Well, you'll just have to explain it to the press as you explained it to me," I said. "You'd have to be a fool to think that anyone could make up a story that preposterous."

"You're a peach, Karen," Archie replied. "A genuine Baltimore peach. Now, I'll be heading back to Hollywood soon. Please, if any reporters call, just tell them it's all a big mistake."

"I will, my darling," I answered. "I will. Hurry home, now."

"Toodles."

I placed the phone back on the cradle and breathed a sigh of relief. It was a short-lived relief, unfortunately, as immediately after I hung up, the phone rang again.

"Karen, this is Elizabeth Dyer from *Zip Shot* magazine. Is it true that your husband is a homosexual?"

Chapter Twenty-One

The Triumphant Return of My Gay Husband,
and My Subsequent Spiral into Madness

Zip Shot never ran the story. Archie and I were the victims of the worst sort of scandal; the sort that is too shocking for newspapers to report. I had to defend myself to countless reporters who never even had the decency to run the story. In those days, you see, homosexuality wasn't the socially acceptable joy ride that it is today. To be accused of being a homosexual was to encounter a stiff wall of silence from the Hollywood community. There were plenty of homos in Hollywood, of course, as there always was and there always shall be, but the policy in those days was "don't ask, don't tell." I don't know why the studios can't put their considerable power to work for a good cause every now and again. If Hollywood chose to do for the homosexual what it did for the cigarette, we'd all be wearing hot pants and roller skates to church on Sunday.

But this has nothing to do with the problem at the time, which is that my husband was a homosexual, even though he really wasn't, even though he really was. As soon as he returned, we got straight back to business, going on a week long bender that would have put Betty Ford to shame. During the day, I stumbled through the end of my shooting schedule on *The Bountiful Good Earth*, and at night, Archie and I boozed it up in the hottest B-list bars in Hollywood. Word of Archie's alleged transgressions spread among the B-list crowd like wildfire.

Everywhere we went, it seemed, we were either being stared at or whispered about or propositioned by some pervert. It was nearly enough to make me say, "Enough! Yes, Mr. Pervert, we will have a roll in the hay with you tonight!"

Poor Archie, the dear was in a sorry state. When he wasn't ripped out of his gourd on wine spritzers he was moping around the house, convincing himself and me that we would never work again. I was not terribly happy myself, having been tossed into the frying pan through no fault of my own. I had always assumed that if anyone was going to destroy my career, it would be me.

On top of all this, I began to develop a rather strenuous washing regimen that took up much of my time. Every morning, I would take three showers, during which I performed the same rituals: lather, rinse, shampoo, rinse, lather, rinse. After lunch, I would go through the process again, and a third time before I went out for the evening. As you can imagine, with all that scrubbing, my skin would sometimes look a spotty mess. I compensated by starting a moisturizing and makeup ritual that would sometimes take up to an hour to perform. All told, five hours of my day became devoted to body care.

Mulgar, as my stylist, was the first to notice my little problem. He was dressing me up for the 1941 RKO Easter Ball, when his hands brushed against a rather nasty scab hiding just beneath my neckline. The scab started bleeding profusely, soaking my dress and Mulgar's hands. Mulgar began screaming like a banshee, convinced that he had broken me. To calm him down, I took off my dress and showed him that my body was entirely covered with raw spots. Unfortunately, the dual shock of seeing me both naked and covered with horrible scabs had the adverse effect of calming him down. He clammed his eyes up tight and began doing loop-de-loops around the room, emitting a high-pitched wail that could have killed a pack of deaf malamutes. With hands outstretched, he ran herky-jerky around the room, smacking into furniture like a pinball caught between bumpers. Finally, exhausted, he toppled over onto his back. I stood over him as he lay deposed on the bedroom floor, gasping for breath and waving his arms and legs in the air.

"Honestly, Mulgar, you look like a retarded turtle," I said. "I've just been feeling a little dirty lately. Now, if you'll excuse me, I have to go take three showers."

A few weeks after the Easter Ball, (which I missed, due to my unfortunate cleansing schedule), I met with my agent, Pauly Auskie. I had a foreboding feeling about this meeting, so I brought Mulgar along with me for moral support. Poor Mulgar was still a little shaken by the Easter Ball incident. When I finally managed to calm him down that night, I swore him to secrecy. No one was to know of my obsessive washing habit, even my husband.

It was not difficult to hide my problem from Archie, as we had not made love since he returned from Hawaii. He began spending more and more hours away from the house, doing who-knows-what with what-knows-whom. He kept his schedule well hidden from me. "Don't worry, my darling," he would say when I asked. "I am making things better for both of us. Be patient."

Patient I was not. In fact, I was feeling rather impatient on the day that Pauly Auskie ushered me and Mulgar into his office, all smiles and handshakes. If there's one thing you can't trust, I always say, it's a smiling agent. I looked at Mulgar, who was a good social barometer. Mulgar returned my look with a deadly serious shake of his head.

"Pauly, you gotta get me work," I said, after we were seated. "I'm dying over here. I'm stuck in that damned house all day, waiting for the phone to ring. I can't bear to let my talents go to waste like this. The people need me, Pauly. They need me."

Pauly had a grim look on his face.

"Karen, I'm gonna level with you. There's no denying that you're beautiful and talented. But you've developed a little bit of a reputation around town. Tom Fancy won't even speak to me anymore after your behavior on *The Bountiful Good Earth.*"

"What is he talking about?" I sniffed. "My performance was flawless! Sure, maybe I tied one on every now and again, but did you see the dailies? It was my finest hour!"

"I saw the dailies, and quite frankly, you looked a mess. Forgetting your lines, slurring through your speeches ... the film is basically dead in the water, Karen. The studio is not happy."

"Oh, poppy twiddle," I replied. "Nothing that can't be fixed in post."

"Let me be perfectly clear, Karen," Pauly said. "Unless you clean yourself up, you will never work in this town again. God knows you're already in enough hot water, being married to a known pervert."

"*Please,* Pauly," I said, "Don't make me laugh. You know as well as I do that Archie is a straight-shooter. He was set up."

"The last time I saw a setup like that was in Bangkok," Pauly quipped. "Your man's a nancy-boy, sure as I'm born."

I suddenly burst into tears. My emotions were out of control in those days, due to my habitual self-medication and general lack of mental stability. Mulgar wrapped his arm around my shoulders. Pauly looked down his nose at us.

"I'm sorry to have to do this, Karen," he finally said, "but I'm going to have to cut you loose."

"No, Pauly!" I wailed. "I'll do better, I promise! I'll stop drinking! I'll show up on time! I'll even leave Archie if I have to. Anything, Pauly. Just give me one more chance."

Pauly shook his head, silently.

I dropped to my knees and started crawling across the floor to him.

"Have you ever made love to a tiger, Pauly?" I asked. "I can fulfill your wildest fantasies ..."

"Karen ..."

I slithered up to his chair and reared back on my knees. I put my hands on his knees and brought my face close to his. He stared at me with a cold expression, his eyes unblinking.

"Meow," I said, seductively.

"For Christ's sake, Karen!" Pauly exploded, grabbing me by the wrists. "Get a grip on yourself! There are children present!"

"There are?" I asked.

Pauly pointed to Mulgar, who was sitting on the edge of his chair and swinging his legs, staring blankly at the wall behind Pauly's desk.

"That is a child, isn't it?" Pauly whispered.

"No, Pauly," I said, shaking my head. "That's Mulgar."

"Oh," Pauly said, clearly disconcerted. "Well, I don't really know from a mulgar, but I do know this: it's time for you to scram."

"Pauly ..." I pleaded.

"Get lost, kid. If you ever kick that monkey off your back, maybe we can chat. But right now, I got no parts for losers."

I knew when I was defeated. I took Mulgar by the hand and, dejectedly, we left Pauly Auskie's office.

With no agent and no hopes of getting another one, I fell into a deep depression. If Archie and I were drinking heavily before I lost my agent, we were now practically bathing in alcohol. Archie continued his mysterious behavior, sometimes disappearing for days at a time. One day blended into another, and before I knew it, two years had passed.

I lost touch with Daddy and Granpapa during my drunken years. Deep down inside I knew that Daddy was concerned, but his response to distress tended toward denial. Granpapa, on the other hand, was becoming somewhat senile in his old age, and he didn't have time to bother with a self-destructive granddaughter who shut herself away from the world with her homosexual husband. Even little Mulgar's visits became less and less frequent. With his sensitive temperament, Mulgar had a hard time seeing me in such a state. He harbored a certain amount of hostility toward my husband, who he blamed for ruining my life and career.

Somehow, the money kept rolling in, despite our lack of work. When pressed, Archie would simply tell me that he'd "made some smart investments." During a period of great sacrifice for the American people, Archie and I continued to spend money without a care in the world. The War was so far outside of our worldview that, frankly, I couldn't even tell you who we were fighting. I know now that we were over in Europe helping the Jews fight the Japs and the Krauts, but at the time I could not have cared less. As long as someone was still distilling grain into alcohol, I was happy as a clam.

It was in the summer of 1943 that I finally received a second chance. I was just about at the end of my rope. The constant boozing and intensive washing regimen took its toll on my skin, and at 21 years old, I could have passed for 40. I had not worked a day since being dropped by my agent, and I was feeling anxious to return to the spotlight.

I was lazing around on the davenport with a glass of bourbon, as was my normal nine-to-five routine, when a rather extraordinary call came in from a producer at Universal.

"Hello, Karen?" the producer said. "This is Clem Gompers from Universal Studios. I'm trying to get in touch with a man by the name of Fletcher Bisque."

At the mention of my ex-lover's name, my heart skipped a beat. My mind was thrown back to that terrible, rainy evening five years prior, when Fletcher was slaughtered so needlessly right on top of me. Just the thought of it made me want to take a nice, long series of showers.

"I'm afraid I can't help you," I said. "I haven't the foggiest idea of where he might be."

"Well, here's the song-and-dance, Karen," Clem Gompers began. "I have just secured financing on a helluva script, a real blockbuster written by a guy named Fletcher Bisque. We picked the script up several years ago but never produced it. Go through the files, make a few calls, turns out no one has heard from Fletcher Bisque in five years."

"So what does this have to do with me?" I asked nervously.

"I do a little poking around, I find the guy's personal information. Turns out the guy was presumed dead some years back. Turns out you're listed in the guy's will as the next of kin."

"I'm sorry, I don't speak Southern," I said. "What does all this mean?"

"What this means, Karen, is that you're gonna make some money."

Arrangements were made for me to visit Clem's office the next day and work out the kinks of the deal. I dropped the phone back on the cradle and sat for a moment in shock. I was overcome by a strange sensation, a feeling somewhere between intense guilt and elation. How could I willingly take advantage of Fletcher's death, when I had been an integral ingredient in the recipe for his murder? On the other hand, if it weren't for me, Fletcher would never have written his script in the first place, as I was the inspiration for the film.

In the end, I decided that all I could do was try the pretzels and, as my dear friend Lil' Suzy Soul was wont to say, put a lil' plum in it.

I told Archie the news when he returned that night. He was overjoyed at our luck. He, of course, knew nothing about my scandalous past, so I simply referred to Fletcher as a longtime family friend. We celebrated that night, as we did every night, by getting drunk.

The next afternoon, I went to the studio and had my meeting with

Clem. There were a number of script changes which he wanted to run by me before I agreed to sign the deal. Originally, the film was called *The Forbidden Fruit*, and it was about a forbidden love affair between an older man and an underage girl. Now, the film was called *My Dog Sal*, and it was about a Saint Bernard in the Alps who finds a buried chest filled with money. I didn't quibble. The dollar amount on the contract was more than enough to make me forget about any artistic objections I may have had. And also, I didn't have any.

I returned home after that meeting feeling on top of the world. My guilt over benefiting from Fletcher's death lasted only as long as my fear that I was getting involved in some sort of police setup. The meeting with Clem was enough to convince me that the studio was on the level. No one knew of Fletcher's murder, and no one really cared. The studio just needed to pay someone on the books so that the government didn't go poking into their business, and that someone was me. Yes, I was feeling a right happy badger when I walked into the living room of my home to see an old friend sitting on the couch.

That old friend was Tony Tarantella.

"Hello, Karen," he said, a lizardy smile on his lips.

"What are you doing in my home, Tony?" I asked, coldly.

"How did your meeting go, Karen?" he replied.

"How did you know about my meeting?"

"Let's just say I'm a silent investor."

"Is that some sort of metaphor?"

"No. I'm a silent investor."

I sat down in a chair and stared silently at Tony. I wanted to know more about his involvement, but I refused to give him the pleasure of knowing that I was interested. If I knew Tony, he'd give up the goods when he was good and ready.

"After you left for Guatemala," he began when he was good and ready, "I did a little research on our friend Fletcher Bisque. Turns out he'd written a script. Turns out it was pretty good. Turns out it was darn good. I knew if I could get it produced, it would be a box-office smash. I could have gone to the studios and gotten them to finance it, but what good would that do me? I wanted a piece of the action.

"But there was a little problem. With the Commander out of

Guatemala, my major revenue stream was cut. United Fruit didn't want to get involved in an international scandal, so they cut me loose. Within a month, I had to put the club up for sale. I had no source of income and bills were mounting."

"Aw, poor guy," I said mockingly. "Poor, sad little gangster."

"I am nothing if not a businessman, Karen," he said, ignoring my jibes. "I took a look at the market, and I said, 'what do people in this town want? What do they need that no one else is offering? And most importantly, what do they need that won't cost me a penny to start?'

"I was pondering these very problems one evening at a dinner party for your old friend the Countess D'arger. Seated across from me at the dinner table were two attractive young homos. Now, I say, live and let live. A man wants to hump another man's pooper, less competition for me."

"You're a real doll, Tony," I said dryly. "A real prince of tolerance."

"As you know, Karen," he continued, "I am consumed with natural curiosity. So I asked these guys, 'how do faggots meet in Hollywood?' You try to pick up a guy in a bar and you're liable to get clobbered. They told me that it's a real pain. So, that's when I hit upon my solution ... an escort service for nellies."

"Terrific, Tony," I said. "You're a gay pimp."

Tony smiled.

"There's a lotta money in anus, darling," he said. "A lot of money. I gotta go where the market takes me.

"Before I could get started, I needed an *in*. I'm a gangster. I don't know anything about homosexuals. So, I tell these guys, if they can help me get my business off the ground, I'll make 'em partners. I made enough money that I could finance the film from which you are about to make a killing."

"That's all well and good, Tony," I said. "But it still doesn't explain what you're doing in my house."

Just then, Archie and Royston walked in the front door.

"Hello, darling," Archie said. "Royston and I were just about to ..."

Upon spying Tony on the couch, he froze.

Tony raised his mouth in a wicked smile.

"Howdy, partners," he said.

Chapter Twenty-Two
The Madness and What Happened After

Like a rubber band, something snapped. I couldn't take it anymore. The drinking, the OCD, the gay husband, the dead-end career-I was done. Everything went black.

When I came to, it was two weeks later, and I was in a hospital. According to the doctors, as soon as I heard the news about Archie's homosexuality, I started screaming and did not stop for an entire week. Tired of and somewhat frightened by my caterwauling, my family called in the men in the white suits, who hauled me off and locked me in the Dorothea Dix Clinic for the Mentally Insane, calming my screams with glorious, non-addictive morphine. After that, I fell into a deep sleep that lasted for another week.

I stayed in the hospital for over two years, finally being released in the fall of the 1945. I had far too many adventures in that hospital to discuss here, but I am pleased to announce that I have saved my journals from this time and will soon be releasing my recollections under the title *The Psycho Diaries*.

I began divorce proceedings from Archie while I was in the hospital. He was more than happy to comply. As crazy as our years were together, I hold no ill will toward Archie. He was a dear man, and although I could not satisfy him sexually, we retained a mental connection and close friendship that lasted for the rest of his life. Like dozens of other men, he had the misfortune of being born a homosexual in a time when homosexuality was simply not an option. He tried his damnedest to be a good husband to me, but as the old saying goes, you can lead a horse to water, but you can't make him want a filly if he's really looking for a stud.

Daddy, Granpapa, and Mulgar picked me up on the day that I was released from the hospital. I had such a feeling of release, walking out of those big brass doors to join my beloved men in the passenger side of Daddy's Packard station wagon. I was 23 years old, living clean, showering once a day, and ready to rejoin the world of the sane.

Archie moved to San Diego with Royston and left the house to me. Immediately, I moved Mulgar in so that I wouldn't be alone in my enormous home. I made a pretty penny on the script of *My Dog Sal*, which was a smash success, so I had more than enough money to finance my creative pursuits. Unfortunately, I had no creative pursuits, and as 1946 began, I was feeling increasingly anxious to get back into acting.

Cassie was kind enough to put me in touch with her agent, Stan Pepperhardy, who signed me immediately. Within weeks, I was auditioning again, and within months, I had secured the female lead in a picture that would become my calling card: *Mr. Brently Goes to Brisbane Holler*.

Shooting for *Mr. Brently* began on March 5 1946. I had the pleasure of working with some of the finest actors to ever set foot in Hollywood, including Gastron McClaritif, Buck Simple, and Battie Pierson. The story was your basic "small-town boy makes good" sort of thing. I played Joan Ballentine, the daughter of a wealthy shipping magnate who falls in love with Croy Bently (Gastron McClaritif). Gastron was an absolute joy to work with. He was, in fact, my first lover after Archie. Where Archie was sensitive and shy, Gastron was bold and adventurous. We once made love in the rafters above the set while the crew played ping-pong below us. Sadly, it was not to last, as Gastron was married and I was a recovering psychopath.

When filming wrapped in the summer of 1946, everything seemed to be going swimmingly. My career was back on track, the war was over, and Mulgar and I were having a whale of a time as roommates. While I was in the asylum, Mulgar had put his skills to work, and he was now outfitting the biggest Hollywood stars with his Latin-inspired fashions. I was incredibly proud of my little friend, the kind of pride that you can only have when you're equally successful in a non-competitive field. Mulgar being Mulgar, he never let success go to his head. We often waited for hours in restaurants trying to get a table, because Mulgar refused to use his celebrity to his advantage. I was not quite as humble, but no one really knew who I was.

On the 14th of June, 1946, I received a visit from the United States government that would change my life forever.

It was a sunny day in Los Angeles, and I remember feeling as though I didn't have a care in the world. Mulgar was reading comic books on the porch and I was swinging in the hammock like the Queen of Sheba, contemplating my next big move. I heard the doorbell ring inside the house.

"Oh, Mulgar, will you get that?" I asked, even though I knew it was fruitless. When Mulgar was involved in his comic books, he would not move to save his own life. Begrudgingly, I eased myself out of the hammock and answered the door.

Standing on my porch was a man in a black suit, holding aloft a piece of paper.

"Karen Jameson Hitler," the man said.

Immediately, I felt a chill creep up my spine. It had been many years since I'd been referred to by my birth name. Ever since the whole Holocaust incident, I had been terrified that the press would learn my true identity and expose me as a near-Nazi in the public eye. I had even gone so far as to send letters to several magazines, pleading them not to reveal my true identity in the pages of their magazines. The letters seemed to really do the trick, for no reporters had called in ages. So, as you can imagine, I was quite disturbed to encounter the man standing on my porch without a photographer or a notepad, referring to me by my God-given name.

"Karen Jameson Hitler," the man continued, handing me the paper, "you are hereby summoned to testify before the Senate Grand Jury about your involvement with the Communist party."

"There must be some mistake," I said. "I'm not a Commie."

"In the eyes of the Lord, you are, ma'am," the man said. "Have a good day, and I hope you rot in hell."

With that pleasant thought, he tipped his hat, turned, and walked away. The encounter left me most shaken. I ran back to Mulgar.

"Mulgar!" I shouted. "I'm being summoned by the Grand Jury!"

Mulgar was too focused on his comic books to pay attention. I hauled off and gave him a mighty slap that woke him from his concentration.

"Mulgar, dammit!" I said. "Listen to me! I'm being summoned by the Senate Grand Jury for being a Communist!"

He shook off the slap and took the papers from my hand. He read through them carefully, while I stood above him, shaking with fear and trying to figure out what I had done to merit such unmeritorious attention. When he finished reading the papers, he removed his glasses and looked up at me.

"Dey sink you Commie," he said.

"I know they think I'm a Commie, Mulgar," I said, impatiently. "But why?"

Mulgar shrugged.

I immediately got on the phone with Dick Friendly, the lawyer who helped me through my ordeal with Archie. His sage advice, for which I paid fifteen dollars an hour, was to appear before the Grand Jury and answer any questions they might have.

A week later, I boarded a plane with Mulgar and Dick and we flew to Washington D.C. for the trial. I was to appear before the House Un-American Activities Committee. Hollywood scholars will note that this was over a year before the infamous Hollywood Ten were to appear before the very same committee and walk away with worldwide notoriety. Although history books have failed to acknowledge me, I am proud to say that I was the very first celebrity ever openly accused of Communism.

I was terrified out of my mind and itching for a fight as I walked through the hallowed halls of Congress. Dick Friendly flitted beside me, abuzz with excitement. This was years before the Red Menace became our nationwide concern, and Dick was convinced that this was a career-making turn for both of us. We prepared for the trial as a prize-fighter might prepare for a prize fight, by punching sides of beef in a warehouse. No, we really didn't. That's just a joke. Not the part about being well-prepared ... that part isn't a joke. The joke is that I would prepare for a Grand Jury inquisition by punching dead cows, because I don't really see how that would help me prepare for my testimony. That's what makes it a joke: that little twist on reality.

A crowd of reporters and spectators were assembled in the Grand Jury room, awaiting our arrival. As I walked in the room, the flashbulbs went crazy. I was looking lovely and psychologically sound in my Mulgar-original dress. I had been practicing my expression in the mirror for a week, and if you ever get a chance to take a look at some of those photos, you'll note that I am projecting an air of calm resolve and solemnity in deference to the seriousness of the occasion.

Or you might see the other pictures from that day, the pictures in which my mouth is hanging open in shock and disbelief. These pictures were taken moments after I entered the courtroom and saw the Commander sitting in one of the rows. His eyes caught mine, and he instantly averted his gaze. And suddenly, it became clear to me: all of this was the Commander's fault. That saucy spic ratted me out to the feds for my brief flirtation with Communism in Guatemala.

The leader of the HUAC was the irascible John S. Wood, and boy, did that old prick have a bug up his ass about Hollywood. I was nothing but a warm-up act, a chance for these guys to hone their chops before going after the real big fish. I was a nobody actress with a juicy past and a disposable future.

For four hours, the Grand Jury drilled me on every niggling detail of my life. They asked me about my birth name, my mother's hoboism, my alcoholism, my relationship with Tony, my trip to Guatemala, my alcoholism, and my time spent at Dorothea Dix. They were trying to build the case that everything was connected to a central core, that my upbringing led me to a career as a communist spy, which subsequently turned me into an alcoholic and a raving loony. No matter how hard they tried, though, they couldn't break me. It was my proudest moment as an American. I got in a few zingers, too, as the transcript shows:

Chairman Wood: Are you suggesting then, Miss Jamey, that in the entire time you spent with Juan Banana, you never discussed politics or felt drawn to work for the Guatemalan Communist party? I find that highly suspect.

Jamey: It is difficult to answer your question, Senator, as I firmly believe that everyone has a little bit of Commie in them. And I have had more in me than most. By that, I mean I've had the penis of a Communist inside me.

Wood: Order! I demand order in the court! Miss Jamey, that sort of talk is simply not permissible in this court!

Jamey: I can't say the word "penis?"

Wood: Say it one more time and I'm declaring you in contempt of court!

Jamey: Forgive me for pressing the issue, Senator Woods, but if I need to discuss male genitalia, what word do you prefer I use?

Wood: We won't be discussing male genitalia.

Jamey: Why am I here again?

And so on and so forth, until they finally let me leave. Thankfully, the Commander had kept some information to himself; namely, my involvement in the murder of Fletcher Bisque. I calmed down considerably when I realized that I was not on trial for murder. Perhaps if I knew then what would happen after the trial, I would have been more concerned about the effect the inquisition would have on my career. But I was still young. I did not yet understand that the world chews you up and spits you out and spanks you with a spatula every time you get a brief glimpse of happiness.

Mulgar and I spent the rest of the day taking in the sights of Washington D.C. Mulgar was as happy as a little pig to see the capital city of the country he loved. Everywhere we went, we were trailed by reporters. The cherry trees were in bloom, the birds were chirping, and it was a glorious day to be alive in the United States of Freedom.

The next six thousand, two hundred and fifty days of my life were not quite so glorious. After the Grand Jury, no one would return my calls. I was not charged with any crime, nor did the Grand Jury ever ask me back again. For all intents and purposes, my name should have been cleared. But, as I discovered, to even be accused of Communist activities was to sign your death warrant in Hollywood. These were touchy times for the studios, and taking a chance on someone like me was simply not in the budget.

Daddy reacted rather harshly to the news. He did not mind that I lied to him about my trip to Guatemala. He was not upset to hear the disturbing details of my relationship with Archie. But Daddy was, if nothing else, a patriot, and the knowledge that I had a fling with a known Communist leader left him devastated. He disowned Mulgar and me, shutting off all communication.

And now we come to a very difficult moment in the telling of my life story. An astute reader will notice that the name of this autobiography is *I, An Actress*. "I" being me, Karen Jamey, and "Actress" being my profession. Sadly, during the period of time from 1946 to 1963, I was not an actress. I do not think anyone would be inclined to read an autobiography entitled *I, Not an Actress*, which is what I'm afraid this book would become if I went through the minutia of my seventeen year hiatus. Sure, I could tell you about the days spent lolling about in the hammock, waiting for the phone to ring. I could tell you about the years spent vainly attempting to secure auditions and being turned away because of my name. But what would that get us? That would get us a very dismal portrait of life indeed, and the message of this book is "life is not dismal." Or rather, my life is not dismal. Yours is probably rather depressing, which is why you're looking to escape through my adventures.

Archie left me with plenty of money, so I did not need to worry about working. But the money was no compensation. If I wasn't acting, I wasn't living. If it helps, you can just pretend that I was dead for seventeen years. To help you understand what this might be like, I shall give Chapter Twenty-Three to Myrna and let her bore you to death.

Chapter Twenty-Three

Myrnas Story

I was born in a tarpaper shack in the hills of
Appalachia. Pappy was a coonskin salesman n' Mama
took care of the young'uns. Pappy learned me to sing.
At night we'd make a fire in our yard n' sing songs
about mountains n' skinnin' coons.

I din't never go to school, 'cause Pappy din't go
fer much book learnin'. Mah school was the school of
life. Me n' mah thirteen brothers n' sisters learned
how to survive in the mountains. I din't act in no
fancy plays or have no fancy love affairs like Karen.
Life weren't no funhouse ride fer people like me. The
closest I ever got to seein' a movie or listenin' to
the radio when I was a young'un was the time that
Pappy clubbed that city slicker who drove up to do
some bird watchin'. He stole the radio out of the
feller's jalopy, too plum ignint to realize that the
durn thing wouldn't work 'less it was attached to the
car. He never gave up hope, though. He'd sit n' look
at that thing fer hours. He knew that it was liable
to spring into action at any minute, n' he din't wanna
miss it when it did.

I weren't much of a looker as a young gal. I took after mah mama, who had a face like a donkey with an overbite. But I was a hard worker, n' when I was thirteen, Pappy got me hitched up to a man named Frank who lived in the city. Frank was a few years older'n me. He was up in the hills one day tradin' with Pappy when he heard me a-wailin' n' a-wogglin' in the backyard. Frank swore he was listenin' to the voice of an angel. He bought me off of Pappy that very day fer three bottles of bathtub gin.

We was married in a civil ceremony that woulda been more civil if Pappy hadn't shown up drunk on bathtub gin. We din't have no honeymoon, me n' Frank, less'n you consider losin' yer virginity pressed up against a bale of hay in a barnyard a honeymoon. I din't.

Frank had big plans fer me as a singin' superstar. He scraped together some money n' recorded a couple of singles when I was in mah late teens. They wasn't nothing great, but they got a few spins on the local radio. Some producer from New York was in town one of the days that they got played, n' he flew me n' Frank out to cut a record. The song went to number one on the country charts, n' purty soon, me n' Frank had more money'n we knew what to do with.

I popped out a couple kids when I was in mah early twenties, n' that put an end to mah recordin' career. Me n' Frank bought a little house in Massachusetts with our savins. Frank din't have nothing better to do, so he went to work at the Tupperware plastic factory. Mr. Tupper din't have much money at the time, so he gave Frank a bunch of stock in the company. We din't care much, we had plenty, n' we din't buy nothing but diapers n' beer anyway. It turned out purty good, though, 'cause now I'm worth millions.

I seen a movie in 1965 that had a durn powerful

impact on mah life. I was 35 years old. I had three kids in high school, two in junior high, n' one in kindergarten. Sometimes I went to the movies when the kids was out at school. One day I seen this movie called Monster Massacre that was really good. There was an actress in it who I thought was durn near the purtiest thing I ever seen. That was Karen Jamey.

I started goin' to all of Karen's movies when they come out. She was great. I wrote to her once n' she sent me an autographed picture. I kept it on the wall of our room until she smashed the frame n' tore the picture up in a fit of drunkenness.

Me n' Frank had a purty borin' life, I guess. One time we went to England n' ate dinner with the Queen, who was a fan of mah music. That was fun. Mah kids grew up to be purty successful. Two of 'em are rock stars, one of 'em is a doctor, one of 'em's a lawyer, n' one of 'em's dead. The littlest one, mah baby, Tansy, is a C.I.A. agent or somethin' like that. I don't see her much, 'cause she's usually off in fur-rin countries assassinatin' dictators n' things.

Mostly, I spent mah time meeting with other Karen Jamey fans. In 1973, I was elected the president of her fan club. That was durn near the proudest moment of mah life. Karen herself was there to present me with mah sash n' tiara.

Frank died off of cancer in the early 80s. It was real hard fer me fer a few years. Real hard. He was a good man n' a good provider. With mah kids all grown up n' out of the house, I decided to sell the house n' take off on a trip 'round the world.

I spent the next five years travelin' 'round the globe, meetin' people from all over the place. It was real nice. Almost no one in other countries had heard of Karen Jamey, though, n' I missed talkin' about her movies somethin' fierce.

When I come back, Karen was lookin' fer a roommate, so we moved in together. We lived in a house fer awhile, but it got to be a little too much fer us to handle, so we moved into this condo together. It's real nice here. The people are real interestin' n' on Fridays we have line-dancin' classes. I got me a lil' cat named Costco who makes me real happy.

Mah kids stop by ever once in awhile, but mostly it's just me n' Karen. She's a purty good person to live with, I ain't complainin'. Heck, it's not too many people who get to live with a real superstar.

I guess mah life's been all right so far. It ain't been excitin' nor jam-packed like Karen's, but I lived a purty good life n' I think the good Lord's gonna provide fer me nice when I reach the pearly gates. Hopefully, all them orphans me n' Frank saved with our charity foundation are waiting up there to put in a good word fer me, or at least the ones that are already dead.

Jesus Christ, Myrna, I asked you to do a chapter not an entire fucking novel! Do you mind?

I sure am sorry, Miss Jamey. I get to flappin' my lips sometimes n' I just don't know when to stop.

You can say that again. Fix me a drink, will you dear? And my God, would you please take off that hideous frock? I can't even look at you. You look like an explosion in a paint factory.

Chapter Twenty-Four

The Lead and How to Swing It

The date was December 26 1963. I was sitting in a diner, contemplating suicide. At 41, my youth had faded and I hadn't worked since being blacklisted seventeen years earlier. Daddy still hadn't talked to me, except for the time he called to tell me Granpapa was dead. I had drifted so far away from Daddy and Granpapa that the news did not affect me very much. In addition, I had a pretty strong morphine habit at the time, which left me unconcerned with the rest of the world. The doctors at the asylum had substituted two addictions for one.

I was not the sort of twitching junkie that you see in the movies, however. I lived a very comfortable life while I was medicated. My doctor kept my prescription active, and instead of using morphine to get high, I used it to stay comfortably numb. Still, enough depression managed to crawl through the haze to make me feel as though the time was ripe for me to make my departure from this mortal coil. It didn't help matters any that I spent the most depressing Christmas of my life with Mulgar the day before. Neither of us felt like cooking or decorating a tree or buying presents for one another or getting dressed, so we spent the day in our underwear on the couch, tossing playing cards into a hat.

As I was sitting in that booth trying to come up with a good suicide plan, two things happened in quick succession that picked me out of my doldrums and set my life, once again, on the right path. The first thing that happened was a song came on the radio that stopped me dead in my tracks, a song by a brand new group from Liverpool called the Beatles. I shouted at the waitress to turn it up, and I listened intently. People say you always remember where you were when you heard that John F. Kennedy died. Well that's poppycock. I wasn't even aware that he was president. But I know exactly where I was when I first heard "I Want to Hold Your Hand." It was as though God himself was smiling down on me, saying, "It will be all right, Karen. Four lovable mop tops want to hold your hand."

When the song came to an end, I burst into tears. All of the pain of the last seventeen years billowed up inside me and came flooding from my tear ducts. At the table beside me, a young gentleman was drinking coffee by himself. When he heard me crying, he rose from his table and slid into the booth across from me.

"Hey, hey, it's all right," he said. "No reason to cry, man."

I looked up into his face. He had long, dark hair, a pencil-thin moustache, and a warm smile. As soon as he caught my eye, his large brown eyes popped open wide.

"Holy shit!" he said. "You're Karen Jamey!"

It was the first time I had been recognized in years. I straightened up and tried to appear dignified.

"Yes, dear, I am," I said, holding my head high.

"Well, Karen Jamey, my name is Handy Peters, and you have a little string of snot coming out of your nose."

I grabbed the napkin off of the table and wiped my nose, embarrassed. Something about the young man made me feel comfortable. It was similar to the feeling I got when I met Mulgar years before. He seemed so warm, and so self-assured, that I immediately dropped my act and opened up like I had not opened to anyone in years.

"Oh, who am I fooling?" I said. "I like you, Handy Peters. I don't know why, but I do."

"I like you, too, Karen Jamey," he said, excitedly. "I've seen all of your movies. My friends and I run a little film series out of a little theater on Wilshire. *The Gates of Poseidon* is a camp classic."

"I think you must be thinking of something else, dear," I said. "*The Gates of Poseidon* is about the Peloponnesian War, not camp."

Handy laughed.

"Oh, Karen, you are too much. Say, Karen, can I ask you a question?"

"Anything, dear."

"Well, I don't want to insult you, but I'm a filmmaker myself, and I would be honored if you'd act in one of my films."

"I'm flattered, dear," I said, "but I haven't acted in years. I'm legally not allowed to. They blackballed me and kicked me out of the union for sleeping with a Communist revolutionary."

Handy ran his finger along his moustache in thought.

"Hmm, that is a head-scratcher, all right. I'll tell you what, why don't you come down to the set anyway? I'm sure we can use you somehow."

With a deal-sealing handshake, we parted ways. I must have looked like a madwoman to the passerby as I ran home, singing "I Want to Hold Your Hand" at the top of my lungs. Well, bully for them, because I was mad. Mad at the world that had denied my existence for so many years. Mad at the studios who tossed me aside when I ran into a few personal problems. Mad at the producers, the directors, the military commanders who had talked me up, dressed me down, told me lies, and treated me like I was yesterday's news before I was ever even allowed to be today's news. I was mad, all right. And fixing to get madder.

I burst in the front door. Mulgar leapt up from the couch, startled at my crazed appearance.

"Mulgar! I got a part! I'm going to be in a movie!"

Immediately, a spark of fire reignited in Mulgar's eyes. He bounced up and down, clapping his hands like a right little seal. I scooped him up off the ground and together we danced around the living room, singing "I Want to Hold Your Hand" at the top of our lungs.

I flushed the rest of my morphine pills down the toilet that evening. Withdrawal was difficult, but Mulgar, thank God, was there to help me through it. The thought of acting again put new life into my cheeks, and within a week I looked ten years younger. Mulgar perked right up as well, his constitution being cosmically tied to mine. He put me on a strict age-reducing regimen based on Guatemalan techniques passed down through the generations. You'd be surprised at how much younger you look after spending a night with your face inside a dead chicken.

The first week of January, Mulgar and I drove out to Handy Peters' studio in San Fernando. We drove straight northwest on the Golden State Freeway, down winding roads to the depths of the valley, down a long dirt path, until we finally got to a rickety old barn in a field overgrown with crab grass and despair.

"This doesn't look so good," I told Mulgar. He nodded in agreement.

I was wearing a beautiful Mulgar original to mark my reentrance into showbiz. Strung around my neck was a lovely mink stole that had been a present from Tony, back in the days before our love turned sour. As I walked to the barn, Mulgar walked behind me, holding the train of my dress up like a royal princess.

The barn doors were propped open wide, awaiting our arrival. A handful of people stood inside the barn. When we got to the transom, they stopped their conversations and stared at us. I lifted my head up high and stared right back at them.

"I.

"Have.

"Arrived," I said, most emphatically, pursing my lips and tossing the assembled spectators a withering glance. There was a brief moment of silence as they drank me in with their eyes. And then, on cue, they all began applauding.

Handy stepped out of the crowd and walked up to us, his face abeam with smiles.

"Karen!" he said, excitedly. "You've made it!"

Handy took me aside and explained the role to me. As I could not legally show my face on camera, I would be playing the monster in the film, entitled *The Creature from Monster Lake*.

"It's the best part!" he said. "You'll have to wear a monster costume, but you really get a chance to emote. The monster, you see, is a metaphor for the government. If this film is going to succeed, it will be on the strength of your performance. You're the only actor in Hollywood who can do it, Karen. We're counting on you."

I'm no fool. I knew he was buttering me up. But it was a welcome change after years of being ignored. "Yes," I told Handy Peters, "I will play this monster. And I will be the best damn monster you have ever seen."

Handy smiled, positively giddy with excitement.

"You heard the lady," he shouted back to his cast and crew. "Let's blow."

We filmed five scenes that day in the barn and around Handy's property. Handy Peters worked fast. I did not have any lines as the monster, but before each scene, Handy gave me careful direction and motivation. My background in blackface taught me how to find the emotion behind the makeup, and I believe to this day that my performance in *The Creature from Monster Lake* ranks among the finest portrayals of a murderous fiend ever committed to film.

Working with Handy was one of the great pleasures of my life. His passion for film was positively inspirational, and he drew a mad cast of characters into his world who shared a like-minded view of the cinema. These were people to whom the magic of movies still mattered. They would scrimp and save to produce a low-budget 16 millimeter film which they would then take around the United States for the enjoyment of other cinephiles. Even on that first day of filming, I felt as though I was a part of something bigger than myself. Call it a movement, call it a pipe dream, call it a waste of time; it was our little slice of Heaven, and we intended to make the most of it.

The Creature from Monster Lake was released in the summer of 1964 to little or no fanfare. Our premiere was held at the Staunton Theater on Wilshire, where Handy and his friends worked during their non-filmmaking hours. The theater was filled with Handy's friends, actors, co-workers and admirers. Here was Jackie Fabulous, the infamous ex-cop turned drag queen who appeared in over 30 of Handy's films. There was Loretta LaRouche, who later achieved some degree of fame for being kidnapped by the Philippines Liberation Society. Over there was Punxsutawney Peter, beatnik icon and friend to such luminaries as Gregory Corso and that fellow who wrote the book about the road.

It was at the after-party that I had a revelation that changed my life for the better. Looking around at the mad crowd of freaks and weirdoes surrounding me, I finally felt at home in the world. These were my people, I realized. My early hopes of becoming a Hollywood leading lady had been crushed by circumstance and poor personal decisions. I spent years bemoaning my fate and trying to wear a dress that simply would never fit me. Well, here was a dress that fit perfectly, a dress made of personal acceptance and inner peace. To these people, I was a super-star. Not because I graced the cover of famous magazines or because I won some petty golden statue, but because I was what I was, am, and ever shall be: a damn fine actress.

At one point in the evening, Handy sat down at the table next to me and gave me a big kiss on the cheek.

"Karen, darling, it has been such a pleasure to work with you," he said, "and I say; S.A.G. rules be damned. You are too beautiful to hide behind a monster mask. I've just completed a script called *Monster Massacre,* and I would be honored if you would play my leading lady."

I clasped Handy's hands and stared deep into his eyes.

"Oh, Handy," I said, "it has been a joy, an absolute joy. I will be your leading lady, Handy. In film, and in life. I do, Handy. I do."

Handy stared back at me, a look of confusion in his eyes.

"Karen, you know I'm gay, right?"

I smiled.

"Well then, Handy, it's best we don't marry. I've been on that merry-go-round once before, and it is no ride I care to go on again. I shall, however, still play the leading lady in your film. I'm sorry I have to let you down this way, but it is, after all, for the best."

Handy laughed and clasped my hands tightly.

"Oh, Karen Jamey," he said, "you are a true original."

"I am, Handy Peters," I replied. "I am."

With that behind us, we settled in for dinner. I had the chowder. And you know what? It was fucking delicious.

Chapter Twenty-Five
Wedding Bells

August 30 1980. I am 51 years old, and I am getting married for the second time. I stand before the church doors, Daddy's arm in mine, waiting to walk down the aisle.

My revelation at the *The Creature from Monster Lake* cast party awakened in me a tremendous desire to set my life straight. I called Daddy for the first time in years. We had a teary reconciliation in the back booth of Mr. Friendlier's. Daddy begged my forgiveness for his untoward behavior, and I was only too happy to oblige. Seventeen years of coldness be damned, a girl is nothing without her father.

My next film with Handy, *Monster Massacre*, was a smash success. We traveled around the country in a great painted bus, showing the film on college campuses, in independent art theaters, and anywhere that would grant us an audience. Mulgar fit right at home with Handy's cast of oddballs, and he would sew mad matching costumes for the entire cast. We were a traveling freak show, in love with ourselves and the universe that loved us right back.

I made a decent living as a regular player in Handy's films throughout the sixties and early seventies. Handy was never accepted by the Hollywood mainstream, but he always turned a profit, and today our films are beloved by an ever-growing cult of admirers.

The one film for which I am most recognized and of which I am most proud is Handy's last film, *Groovy Business*. I played Ms. Bopeep, an evil Hollywood madam who oversees a bordello full of vampires. It is universally acknowledged that I carried the film with my performance, and to this day I receive letters from new fans telling me they absolutely despised me in the film.

Handy passed away in 1975, the victim of too many years of partying and too few friends with CPR training. We tried in vain to resuscitate him the night of his death, but with no knowledge of mouth-to-mouth, the best solution we could come up with was to beat him about the chest with sticks. This, we discovered, does not help.

His funeral was a joyous affair, much like Granny's funeral years before. Everyone who met Handy fell in love with him, and his funeral was attended by hundreds of the filthiest, most lovable dirt bags you would ever want to meet. We all got blitzed on horse and had a smashing good time saluting our old friend and mentor.

After that, I made a steady living in soap-operas, commercials, and the like. I was never a marquee star, but I am well-known enough by the people who know things well. The great film critic Pauline Kael once called me "a true survivor," which is nicer than anything she's ever said about Woody Allen.

And now, here I am, as giddy as a little schoolgirl in Sex Ed. Inside the church, the organist plays the opening chords of "I Want to Hold Your Hand." Cassie, my matron-of-honor, turns around and smiles back at me, as if to say, "We've been through a lot, kid, but it looks like we've finally made it." I smile back, as if to say, "Yes, and thank you for not ruining my wedding, as I ruined several of yours."

Finally, it is our turn to walk down the aisle, and away we go. I scan the pews full of friends and well-wishers and I am greeted by warm smiles and gentle tears. I nod to everyone who meets my eye, welcoming them into my happiness.

Mulgar stands at the altar in an adorable tuxedo he built himself. His little face beams with joy and excitement. He appears to have gotten over the intense vomiting spell that had him laid up all morning.

I take his tiny hands in mine and stare deeply into his eyes. We recite our vows. When it comes time, Mulgar says, proudly and distinctly, "I do." For so many years, this has been his only desire, and now,

I am here to fulfill it. He is the only man who has stuck with me through thick and thin, and for that, I will always love and admire him.

"I do," I say, when we get to that part of the script. I say it in a sweet, low voice, a voice that positively drips with sincerity that falls from my mouth and fills the church, captivating the audience and performers alike. After all these years, I am finally who I was always meant to be: Mrs. Mulgar Blotz.

It is the greatest performance of my life.

Epilogue

In 1997, we buried Mulgar under an oak tree in Hollywood Forever Memorial Park. He actually died of hyperactivity in 1981, a few months after our wedding. We kept his body cryogenically frozen for many years, until I realized that cryogenics was a bunch of nonsense and a real drain on the old coffers.

We managed to carve a jolly good time out of those few months of marriage. Giving Mulgar his first real taste of woman was perhaps the noblest thing I shall ever do. I was greatly saddened to see him go. Really, this entire autobiographical experience is in tribute to the dear little man who changed my life forever. More than that, it is a tribute to me.

I continued working throughout the 80s and 90s in a string of bit parts. From cable television series to cracker commercials to local theatrical productions, I've run the gamut of showbiz. I am thankful and grateful that I've been able to sustain a living as an actress without getting too roughed up. I've taken my lumps, that's for sure, but I always come back fighting.

Myrna and I moved in together in the early 90s. At first, we lived in the house, but we really didn't need all that room, so we moved into this condo, where we live today. Although she can be somewhat of a ninny, she pays her share of the rent and we have a nice time playing canasta and watching television. It's a pleasant enough life for an old woman who has had her fair share of excitement.

I travel quite often to do personal appearances at film festivals and conventions. My audience is very loyal, if a bit insane. Still, it is nice to be admired, even if your admirers tend to be 40-year-old men who still live in their mothers' basements.

I still act whenever I get a chance. This year alone, I will be appearing in a few major releases, including *The Cost of Living*, *The Bride of Trash*, and *Vengeance: America*. My roles tend to be small, but I am happy to have them all the same.

Daddy is still alive. I had to put him into an old folk's home a few years back, which was quite a painful decision for me. The women who run the home treat him very well, though, and he always has a smile for me when I visit.

As I speak these words, I am staring at a lovely robin sitting on a bough of the cedar tree outside my window. I feel as though I should be able to say something meaningful about this robin that leaves you with hope for the future, but I cannot. The robin is brown. I am an old lady. Life is too short. Grab your robins when you can, or they just might fly away.

That's not bad. Perhaps in my next life, I shall become a poet.

Fuck literature.

www.contemporarypress.com

Current Titles

Dead Dog by Mike Segretto: A curmudgeonly shut-in's life is turned inside-out when he becomes involved with a trash-talking femme fatale, a trio of psychotic gangsters, and a dog whose incessant barking has caused him years of sleepless nights. Spiked with ample doses of sex, violence and campy humor, *Dead Dog* is a riotous road trip from an Arizona trailer park to hell.
ISBN 0-9744614-0-7

Down Girl by Jess Dukes: In *Down Girl*, 29-year-old Pauline Rose Lennon works too hard for every cent she ever made until she meets Anton, willing to give her more cash than she's ever imagined...for one small favor. Pauline's life spins hilariously out of control, but she pulls it back from the brink just in time to prove that just because you're down, it doesn't mean you're out.
ISBN 0-9744614-1-5

Johnny Astronaut by Rory Carmichael: In the future, disco is king. *Johnny Astronaut* is the story of a hard-boiled, hard-drinking P.I. who stumbles upon a mysterious book that changes his life forever. Caught between a vindictive ex-wife, a powerful crime boss, and a sinister race of lizard people, Johnny becomes embroiled in a fast-paced, hilarious adventure that stretches across space and time.
ISBN 0-9744614-3-1

G.O.P. D.O.A. by Jay Brida: While the city braces for 20,000 Republicans to descend on New York, a Brooklyn political operative named Flanagan uncovers a bizarre plot that could trigger a Red, White, Black and Blue nightmare. Populated by buffoons, hacks, thugs and the Sons of Joey Ramone, *G.O.P. D.O.A.* is a fast paced, ripping yarn that gorges on the American buffet of sexual hypocrisy, political ambition and the Republican way of life.

ISBN 0-9744614-5-8

How To Smash Everyone To Pieces by Mike Segretto:Ex-stunt woman, mass murderer, and champion wise-cracker Mary is furious to discover that her twin sister Desiree – accused of murdering her husband – has been wrangled back to an Arizona prison by a grizzled detective named Tuttle. Fueled by an unnaturally obsessive love for her twin, Mary sets off on a homicidal cross-country campaign to free Desiree from the clutches of the law, recruiting a bizarre bunch of cohorts on the way.

Exploding with action, uproarious one-liners, and more cartoon violence than an episode of Tom and Jerry, How to Smash Everyone to Pieces is one of the most perverse and hilarious tales ever to come tearing down the highway.

ISBN 0-9744614-6-6

contemporary press

Contemporary Press (est. 2003) is committed to truth, justice and going our own way. When Big Publishing dies, we're the cockroaches who will devour their bones and dance on their graves.